LEE WHIPPLE

No Fool I

QUILL POWER PUBLISHING
ASHEVILLE, NC

No Fool I

This book was printed by Lightning Source, Inc., a print on demand publisher.

This book is a work of fiction. The characters, incidents, and dialogue are drawn from the author's imagination and are not to be construed as real. Any resemblance to actual events or persons, living or dead, is entirely coincidental.

Printed in the United States of America

ISBN #: 978-0-615-35091-2

About the Author

Lee Whipple graduated from Georgia Tech with a Bachelor of Civil Engineering. He loves to write songs on guitar and play them for audiences. He likes to draw architectural renderings occasionally. He likes to play basketball although he is too old and slow.

Lee is a sharp chess player, and hopes to reach a USCF rating of 2000 someday. He loves dogs although he does not have one. He feels the best way to write a book is to set aside some time every week to write regularly.

The quotations at the beginnings of each chapter are from a book of selected quotations. I have not read most of the books from which they were taken.

This book is available to order from Amazon and Barnes and Noble. Bookstores may order this book through Ingram.

❖ Chapter 1

"Music hath charms to soothe the savage beast, to soften rocks, or bend a knotted oak."
William Congreve, The Mourning Bride

It didn't seem so hard at first. Once there were friends to be had just by raising your head and looking around the room. I'm talking about in school, where you couldn't hardly move without bumping into someone. Even the ones who thought they were alone really weren't. Shoot, I was one of them. And I didn't have the smarts or the courage to get involved with a nice girl at that point. Later, when I did have the courage, I still didn't have the smarts to hold on to one. So, I left college to be alone. The farther away school got, the harder it was to meet someone. Shuffling around from town to town, sometimes it seems as if you were shuffled. But a card wouldn't be alone in a deck, would it? I mean, stacked in there with all those other similar cards? One right on top of the other.

I looked up from my video game on my laptop. It wasn't every day that I was on a plane, so I wanted to take in every last detail. The flight attendant had just turned to face the passengers, and the seat belt lights had come on.

"We are approaching our destination everyone," she explained. "Please remain seated until the plane comes to a complete halt. Thank you for flying with us."

Between the passengers and the pilot, I knew there was a solid bulletproof wall that was the result of numerous past hijackings. It also blocked signal from all of the passengers' digital phones so they wouldn't interfere with the cockpit radio. I was also able to use my laptop to access the internet, a service provided by the airline. While I had been distracted by the stewardess, my character in the game had been hunted and killed, so I bowed out gracefully. Then, I fastened my seat belt and turned my attention to the window.

For a while, there was nothing to see but clouds. The plane passed under these though, and tiny features were visible. The roads and cars looked unreal, the houses like toys. The window was a TV locked on to a fairy world separate from the reality of the plane. Then came groups of buildings from the city. Still unreal. But slowly, by degrees, the scale of the outside world came to match ours in the plane, and reality intruded as we landed. Then we hooked up to the passenger walkway.

I had already put my laptop in my shoulder bag. People were jockeying for position to see who would be the first in the aisle, the first off the plane. Hurry up and wait. We had all shared what should have been an amazing experience. There had been some small talk. But now, we were to be separated again. There was no talking in the line. We moved off the plane like cattle. A few had people waiting for them, a happy reunion. Most just made their way to the luggage carousel, to wait in silence once again. The group that included the passengers of the plane spread out and thinned like fog into the city, to forever be separated. Modern transportation can take us anywhere.

I was no exception. Once I got my luggage (a suitcase and a large backpack), I rented a car and headed for a motel near town. Usually motels near a city are fairly safe. It's the rural motels that you have to watch out for. No one can control what goes on out there. Of course, all motels as a rule are something to stay away from, unless you're trying to score something. But I didn't have anywhere to go until I could find an apartment. I had broken a lease at my last place. Boy, there's another thing you don't want to do. They fined me two months rent. Some of that had to go on my credit card, along with the plane tickets. Things were not looking too good for me financially, but at least I had a job to look forward to. Something nice, in the city. I decided to dump my luggage at the motel and go out on the town to celebrate.

*　*　*　*　*

I always love driving downtown to find somewhere to go out. You find on the map where a good-looking neighborhood might be, or you find someone to tell you where the good places to go out are located. Then you drive around carefully and slowly, finding the areas that look interesting. I don't crane my neck around too much, that's asking for an accident. Then, if you drive through a place that looks interesting, look for a place to park on the way out. Don't worry about walking a little ways. It is better to walk than try to turn around and go back through the strip. Unless you want to pay to park, which is also fine.

I was not really willing to pay to park. I had my nice new job, but as I have already said, I was riding some debt. I found what looked like a nice neighborhood commercial strip and parked just beyond it, at a bank. Banks are the best place to park at night, because they're never open. I locked the car and started walking to the strip.

As ZZ Top says, "Sharp dressed man." I had a pair

of designer black slacks on, a red silk shirt, and an all black tie. No top hat though. The wind was blowing my hair around a little bit, but my tie was held in place by a tie clip. Nobody else seems to wear a tie clip these days, but I like them. They are getting a little hard to find in shops, except for antique shops, and I keep losing them as well.

I decided to walk past all the bars and closed shops first. Couples passed me, groups passed me. I didn't pay much attention to them. When you go to a new place, it seems like you almost have to go out at once to make your presence felt. This new strip looked like an interesting place to hang out. First, there was a furniture shop, mostly displaying futons and lamps. Then a lit up alley beckoned me to other closed shops: clothing shops, galleries. I didn't venture into the alley. I passed a sports bar. I passed up an Irish bar. Next there was a club with two levels, and the top had a deck as well. The top level had a band playing somewhat original music. There wasn't too much more to the strip, so I decided to go in.

The man working the door looked at me and said, "I.D." My wallet was already on the way up, and I flipped the driver's license. The man looked at it fairly casually and said, "five bucks." I gave the man a five and he stamped me on the back of my right hand. A few people had stopped and waited behind me, talking together. They laughed and seemed happy to have decided on a place. I tried not to pay attention to their conversation too carefully. I slid past the doorman and on to the bar. The corridor actually pushed into the center of the club, and I was disoriented. People leaned against the walls in groups, but the exit to the corridor spilled me near to a bar. That one was fairly

11

crowded, but I headed toward the most open spot I could find. There's a rule about drinking and driving I have: I don't do it. I don't even start to do it. It doesn't cover for anybody, it just doesn't make sense. Since I was alone without much money, I ordered a cranberry juice when I got to the bar. The yuppie-looking bartender was busy, and looked faintly pissed, but I tipped him a dollar for a dollar fifty drink, so he just turned to other customers. That's another good bar rule.

Don't stop reading now on account of all these rules. I like keeping my life in harmony with others, and I've found these little rules make things easier. The tipping rule is at least a dollar or two for any drink you buy in a bar. There are some places you can go where the drinks are so expensive that a bigger tip for a drink is required. Maybe in an expensive place when you order a complicated mixed drink, you might think about tipping two or three dollars. I don't drink mixed drinks anyway. I feel that they are kind of dangerous. With beer, it is easy to regulate your buzz with just how many beers you drink. With mixed drinks, you could easily drink them fast in an exciting environment. They also vary in strength depending on the bartender. If you're some beautiful girl, he might use a heavy hand to get you a little looser. That seems like a dirty trick to me, but spending your time out in bars really isn't a joke.

So back to the cranberry juice and the lower level of the establishment. I started walking around alone, just to get the feel of the place. I noticed the bathrooms and filed their location away for future reference. Some of the groups of people were dressed nicely as I was. They seemed to congregate mostly between lights that had elegant hand fans covering them, showing illuminated Japanese patterns. Overall, it was a very dark, but there were strips of white neon in different places. A few couches were scattered in one alcove. I saw the stairs that led up to the upper level, but the music had stopped overhead a few minutes ago, and people were starting to crowd down the stairs.

I turned away from the stairway, knowing there would be another band. It was too early for the whole show to be over. I started threading the crowd, riding like a surfer at the crest of the crowd coming downstairs. Then I noticed a couple of girls talking to each other ahead of me. The only one I really saw had wavy blondish hair. It didn't look authentic, but I don't know anything about that. What I do know is that she stood gracefully with a slim full figure. I also know that she had glanced my way as I had approached. I walked straight up to her and looked straight into her eyes. Her friend broke off talking for a moment. I made the best of the opportunity.

"You have a real grace to your stance. It is truly a thing of beauty."

She tilted her head a little bit and looked at me out of the corner of her eye. "Oh, it's the product of years of finishing school."

"Well, the finished product is alluring, I must say. What's your name?"

"Cindy," she said, "and this is my friend Aliana."

I was torn at that moment. I didn't want to break eye contact with her for a second, or start over with a new conversation with her friend. I decided to stay the bold course and keep looking straight at her. "It's wonderful to meet you both. Can I get you both a drink?"

Cindy looked a little annoyed. She raised her glass and showed it to me. It was about three-quarters full. "I don't think so," she said.

Aliana broke in though. "I'll take another tequila sunrise."

"Okay," I said, meeting her eyes for the first time. "Stay right here now, I'll go get it." My cranberry juice needed refilling anyway. I turned away and made the old approach to the bar again. Not too much later and ten dollars poorer, I turned away from the bar and looked for the girls. I've had girls leave after sending me for drinks, but I'm still a sucker for trying to spend a little more time with someone new. It's even worse for a girl to take the drink and just turn away without talking to you. It happens. Luckily, the girls seemed to be in about the same area. I headed back toward them, and I wondered if they had discussed me in the interim.

"One tequila sunrise for Aliana, and I can do nothing for Cindy." I was looking at Aliana this time. She was a little shorter and had very straight black hair. She was wearing one of those tops that has only one strap over one shoulder. Sometimes heavier girls with pendulous breasts wear those things, but Aliana wasn't heavy at all. Just something about her face seemed kind of plain.

"I've never been to this place before," I said, "In fact, I've never been to this city before. Who's playing upstairs?"

Cindy looked a little surprised. "You've never been to ------? What, are you just passing through?"

"No, no. I just got a job here working as a computer network administrator." Aliana pantomimed a

14

yawn. "That sounds like really exciting and creative work."

I frowned. "Well it's a really tough field right now, so it means that I'm damn good at it."

She laughed at me. "I knew I could get under that cool exterior." Cindy joined in the laughter softly.

I smiled a little. "Okay, that was one for you." I looked toward the stairway. "How about going upstairs to see the next band?"

The two girls glanced at each other. Cindy shrugged. "Fine, The Dugouts should be playing soon." We walked in line; Cindy, Aliana, and I, up to the next floor. We pushed through the double doors. Nothing could prepare me for what I was about to experience.

*   *   *   *   *

Curtains blocked off the view of the top floor at first, but I pushed through them into a wonderland. The first thing I noticed were the clouds of fog floating around. At all levels, colored fog drifted slowly about the room. It seemed that lights mounted on the ceiling followed these clouds to light them in soft greens, blues, yellows, and reds. The band wasn't even playing! In fact, there was hardly anyone in the room to appreciate the amazing effects. Next, I noticed streams of colorful ribbons floating through the air. These ribbons were not just falling and twisting down, they were darting in between the clouds like air snakes. They seemed to gather in certain places as if they could converse together, but always moving, moving.

Cindy and Aliana started into the room as if there were nothing out of the ordinary, but I was stunned for a moment. I saw a simple bar to my right along the back wall, and then I looked to my left and saw the stage. Considering the fog and streamers, it looked fairly mundane. There were lights and speakers, but it was mostly colored black. People moved around the stage setting up for what I assumed were The Dugouts. The girls had headed toward the stage, so I followed them. They stood right next to it, with the floor of the stage reaching about chest high. As I came up to them, they sort of turned away, and Aliana reached up to one of the people. There was a quick handshake and the girls turned back to me. Aliana was all smiles, and they both got close into my personal space.

"Look here, now." She opened her palm to show us, and a few reddish green herbs were revealed.

Cindy put one into her mouth immediately and turned to me. "Do you want one?"

I hesitated. "What are they?"

She smiled coyly. "Magic herbs, dummy." I reached out quickly and took one. I chewed it up and swallowed it.

Aliana put one in her mouth and then looked at me with concern. "You didn't swallow that did you?" My stomach turned a little, and I must have looked nervous, because she continued. "You did? Wow!" Cindy and Aliana looked at each other and giggled.

Cindy put a hand on my chest. "You might want to go easy on the alcohol for the rest of the night." We all moved away from the stage. I felt no compunction to tell them that I wasn't drinking anyway. Some more people were starting to enter the room, and the bar was getting busy. We didn't need drinks but moved in that direction anyway. Just something about feeling more comfortable in a crowd, I guess. My mind started to wander, and I looked up at the light show above us again.

The lights made the moving clouds of fog glow warmly. The shapes of the clouds changed slowly as the ribbons swam around them. Then I saw a sparkling rainfall from the clouds above. It seemed that the clouds were raining very slow tiny lights that blinked on and off. They slowly fell to the floor and winked out like sparks falling into a lake. I could feel a grin start upon my face, and it became fixed in place. My face began to flush with the beauty of it all. Cindy and Aliana were also engrossed with the colors and lights. The room was getting more crowded. At that point, two things happened at once.

The lights in the room lowered for the band to come on. Also, a small group of young men who obviously knew Cindy and Aliana came up. Hugs were passed all around, and one of the boys monopolized Cindy. "We're going to a wish party, girls. Just rounding up some stragglers."

Cindy started looking coy again. "Oh, and I suppose we're stragglers, right?"

The boy shook his head in negation. "Whatever you are, you're invited to come, but we're leaving now."

Cindy and Aliana looked at each other and decided. "Of course we will go."

Aliana looked at me. "You should come with us." Cindy looked away at one of the boys. If Cindy had asked, maybe my life would have taken a different course, but sometimes I can be selfish.

"Normally I would, but this concert seems kind of special right now. I'd hate to leave. Plus this light show is really neat." A roar went up from the crowd, now packed in the room. The boys were starting to leave. Cindy was going as well, but Aliana backed away from me to follow them more reluctantly. "You have to come with us! We need to stay together. Don't you?" She was edging away with them.

I smiled and waved goodbye. "I'll be fine! You guys have been great!" I turned to the stage to watch the band. They had walked onstage and picked up their instruments. Without seeming to see each other, they started the first song. They moved in concert, arching forward to the heavy beat. White lights shone from behind them, but didn't stay in a straight line as you would expect. Instead, the light flowed between them and poured down over the front of the stage. For some reason, I felt drawn to the area in front where the light was pooling. I had to snake my way through dancing, jumping fans. A stray arm lashed out and spilled my cranberry juice to the floor. I hadn't yet reached the front of the stage, when I saw that the light that spilled over The Dugouts was pooling on the floor like mercury. The light formed ponds and slid randomly. When someone stepped on it, the light broke into smaller ponds and moved on the floor. No one seemed to pay much attention to this effect. Everyone was too intent on the stage and the band in front of them.

I amused myself for a while by jumping in the puddles of light. To break a fluid light without any discernable splash was truly entertaining. Soon, the band captured me again. The low rhythm pounded from the floor, and the guitars slowly peaked up and down. The singer was pumping his fist out at the crowd, and he sang of dead things animated by strange magical forces. The music was a heavy industrial groove. Typically, though, that scene brings a very select crowd. The people jumping to this band were more diverse. Most people don't jump around in a bar for the reason that jumping tends to spill any alcohol they may have bought.

The Dugouts finished a song, and the crowd cheered wildly, almost uncontrollably. The singer stepped back a few paces, and the white lights faded, dimming and petering out like water from a hose. In the darkness, the guitar players started a slow song, and all the red fog started to move toward the stage. As the band played slowly, the fog collected on the stage and pulsed in time to the music. Then, the tension mounted, and the singer made a few leaps toward the front of the stage. The music crashed out, and showers of individual red sparks shot straight up between members of the band. The singer nodded his head and sang of misspent youth and finding eternity through progeny.

At first, the red sparks faded as they reached higher. But then, after a time, the sparks brightened and curved out to the audience. The brighter sparks wove between crazed dancers. I saw one hit a large dreadlocked man. His chest burst into flames. He shouted out in release, with what seemed like joy. His dancing grew even more frenzied. I glanced back at the singer, who had a sly smile on his face like he knew and approved. Other people were getting hit with sparks and bursting into flames. I myself had been dancing unaffectedly, but I was starting to get a little nervous. I decided to move toward the exit, hoping that the sparks would avoid me entirely.

I danced and weaved through the crowd. The motives were different. I looked for a way out. The sparks found enthusiastic victims. The exit was in front of me.

The curtains parted between my hands, and a roar went up from the crowd. I stumbled down the steps to the first floor. The room was even darker than before, but vertical white neon bars still hummed on the walls. Amazingly, the first floor was mostly empty. I made my way to the center of the room for another cranberry juice. I thought that my feet were tracing a fairly straight line, but there seemed to be zones of invisible pressure that pushed me about as I went to the bar. The white neon on the walls started to ooze sideways

My hands reached out. My first thought was to clasp the bar for support, but even that was not to be. I felt dragged from the center of the room. The white neon bars were bent into "C's" moving faster, but with great momentum. I staggered backwards for awhile, and then I turned. None of the bartenders or patrons seemed to notice that anything was wrong. I should have been afraid, but I was filled with some kind of mellow courage. I searched for something to use as a goal: Chairs, groups of people, another bar. Only the exit seemed to suit. I straightened up quietly, and walked straight to the exit. The invisible forces seemed to withdraw slowly, and I nodded to the doorman as I made my way out.

The street welcomed me as I turned back in the direction of my car. I walked confidently down the street, head held slightly high. Pieces of the pavement started to glitter as I made my way along the shops. The mannequins leered at me out of the corner of my eye, but as I turned to look, they stood innocently. I was loath to speed up my stride, but I yearned for the safety of my car. As I walked along, I noticed something else. The parking meters were getting taller. They seemed to have sharp spines radiating out from the tops. The spines were metallic and shiny. I walked and walked, and the street began to darken. It started to curve in a way that I could not recall. Suddenly, I was less sure of the location of my car. In fact, I didn't remember a curve at all. I began to run in a panic. The streetlights seemed dim and far away. The friendly storefronts turned into darkened doorways. I ran randomly, down side streets I had never seen before. I turned down one alley and came to a stop at a brick wall. My head bowed to rest on the wall, and I pounded it with my fist. I turned around and gasped. Brick enclosed me on all four sides. I was trapped! I looked up, but the walls seemed to reach to infinity. The darkest part of the night had been reached, and I started to shiver. I curled up in one of the corners of my impossible cell and tried to stay warm. The ground stole the warmth from me, but eventually I slept.

❖ Chapter 2

"Those who bring sunshine to the lives of others cannot keep it from themselves."

Sir James Matthew Barrie, A Window in Thrums

I was shocked awake by a cold numbness to my head. There was a burbling all about me, and from the wetness in my hair, I realized my head was lying partially in a stream. I jerked my body away from the water and slid up the bank of the small brook. I shook my head like a dog shakes his body to dry it. I used my sleeve to give my face a few wipes. My breathing was heavy as it can be when you are startled awake from a deep sleep, though I had no idea how I could have fallen asleep with my head in water. I looked about.

There were trees and bushes all about me. None of the vegetation was very large, or for that matter, too thick to travel through. Hills sloped gently up from the stream. I saw no indication of a real trail in any of this wooded area. All was carpeted equally by leaves. It was early morning, and very chilly. I still had on my red shirt, black tie, and black pants, though they were now somewhat soiled. I could think of no explanation of how I had come to this place from the middle of the city.

"Perhaps," I thought, "this is some park that I have stumbled on to." But an unnerving sense of displacement followed this thought immediately. What the hell could have happened? I tried to find the best direction to take. Eventually, it seemed easiest to follow the stream downstream. There was a space at the top of the bank that seemed to be easy going, so I started off. The trees passed me by in perspective. The close trees moved by faster, while the farther ones took longer to pass. Occasionally, I passed trees that had fallen, their dried branches tangled with the living brush. There was a clearing carpeted with low fern, very lovely. But hanging above me was the disquieting feeling that I didn't really know where I was, or where I was going.

Just past the fern clearing, I glanced back one time to get a last look at the fern, and I thought I saw a sort of disappearing movement. I peered through the trees intently, but there was no further movement. This did nothing to ease my mind, but I decided to put the movement down to small wildlife. But had it been staring? I continued along the stream.

Mile after mile. The stream became incrementally larger as small trickles of water fed into it. I drank several times, though I had heard that it was dangerous to do that in the woods without a filter. Finally, the sun began to set, and light faded. I had reached no hint of civilization, and was wondering if I had somehow gone in the wrong direction. There was no way I was going to turn around. Staying in the same place seemed stupid, as there was no one who would be looking for me. I was very hungry, but not yet desperate enough to eat any old mushroom or berry. I had eaten some blackberries that I had found. These had not assuaged my hunger pains at all. I decided to pack it in for the night while I could still see.

I chose a spot near a downed tree so I wouldn't have to go far to get wood. I cleared dead leaves away from a spot and thought of building a fire there. Even though I was weary from walking all day, I retrieved a few stones from the river to contain the fire. Then I tried to start it. I did have my lighter, as always. As the temperature dropped, I praised the fact that I always carried one. I put some leaves down first, with some very small twigs. It seemed like it would be easy enough, but the leaves wouldn't catch well, even when I held the lighter on so long that it burned my thumb. The little pile smoked and fizzled. I knocked it apart in disgust and tried again. This time, I took the time to pick the filmiest leaves and tiny dry twigs, which I made into a teepee. It caught well, and I added wood piece by piece until it was burning brightly.

By this time, night had truly fallen, and the fire was a source of comfort and warmth. There was nothing to do but stare at the fire as darkness reigned. It was still early, but I was tired from the long walk. I knew that the ground was the worst way to have cold stolen from your body, so I piled leaves near the fire so I could lie down. I could imagine bugs and worms in the leaves as I lay atop them. The ground was hard and not warm enough from the fire. It took me a long time to get to sleep.

*   *   *   *   *

I awoke shivering. I was freezing to death. The sky was barely lit, early morning still far away. I sprang to my feet and rubbed my arms and legs. I even jumped around until I stopped shaking. But when I took the time to look around, I was miserable. The prospect of another day felt like a weight upon my head. A long way off, there was a miserable howling that echoed my mood. I relieved myself on a bush, and took stock of my campsite. Strangely, I didn't want to leave. But, as I needed to keep moving to stay warm, I started along the stream bank right away.

Mile after mile. The sun rose, warming me. The hike became pleasant. If only I could stop thinking about food. Then, I was faced with a decision. The vegetation at the stream's edge had turned to brambles. These were almost impassable. I had no idea how far they continued. If I wanted to continue to follow the stream, I would have to be in it. To my left, there seemed to be a small trail going up a hill. I thought that this trail might cross a road, or at least get me to the top of a hill where I could see something. I followed the trail.

Back and forth it went across the hill. In places, rocks protruded into the trail. As I climbed, energy leached out of me in the form of sweat. Very soon I realized that water was going to be a problem. Often, I yearned for a sip of water while the creek was nowhere near. I broke off a piece of straight stick to help me climb the hill. It seemed now to be more of a mountain. I had to duck through the branches of a stand of pines. The path seemed to lead constantly upward, so I felt I would be able to see something soon. But the hill kept going farther and farther up. At times it would seem I was just about to get to the top, only to turn a corner and see yet another climb. Finally, the path rounded off and became more of the top of a ridge. I could see a clearing ahead of me and it looked as if I would be able to see a long way around from there.

Suddenly, the feeling came again that someone was watching me. I glanced quickly to my left and thought I saw a face. It was not behind a tree, but actually in a pine's trunk. The face seemed bearded and old. The bark closed up over it, and I heard words as it faded away. "The forest is endless here." Never in my life had nature handed me such a surreal occurrence. Nature is often variable and unpredictable, but I had never thought of it as sentient. I was so close to the top of the mountain that I decided to finish my journey.

I entered the clearing, and immediately my gaze was drawn to a large black form lying in the middle. It was a wolf, the size of which was truly astonishing. There was no question that this animal might be a dog. The animal exuded an aura of ferocity. It was obviously hurt badly. My first thought was how hungry I was. I thought that I could kill and eat the wolf. Then I realized I had no knife, or way to skin the animal. As if my thoughts were a pendulum, I felt shame overcome me. I felt sorry for the poor creature and examined it more closely.

The wolf's head was large and narrow towards its snout. The legs were long, and one of the front legs was badly broken. That was where all the blood was pooling. The wolf's chest was rising and falling somewhat erratically, and it looked at me out of its near eye. It must have weighed 300 pounds. I stepped closer and it growled weakly.

"Easy, boy," I said, "I'm going to try to help you." Then, once again, I was surprised by nature.

"…water." The wolf said weakly. I stepped back a pace. It was almost as if the act of the wolf talking scared me more than the wolf itself. I had no idea how I was going to get this wolf any water. It seemed to me that the broken leg was a more pressing problem.

"Water." The wolf insisted. I had two ideas simultaneously. One was to try to carry the wolf on my shoulders down to the creek. This seemed unlikely to succeed and dangerous to the wolf, if not myself. The other idea was to go back to the creek and soak my shirt and bring it back to the top of the mountain. This is what I decided to do.

"I'll be right back, wolf. I'm going to get some water for you." Before I left the top of the hill, I took my first look around. There was plenty of room through the sparse trees to see in every direction. The forest was endless. As far as I could see there was nothing but trees. Trees to every side of the mountain, and more hills all around. There was no sign of civilization. No power line or fire tower, nothing. I sighed in resignation and started back down the hill.

The trip down was easier than the trip up. It was almost like a leisurely stroll, only I had to watch my step carefully. I was still thirsty, though. I made it back through the pines to the creek after a short time. I took a long drink and sat down. Then the bearded face surfaced in the bark of a nearby tree. It spoke again. "The forest is more powerful than you imagine, but only you can make it forever." It gazed at me placidly.

I was puzzled. "How can I get out of this forest?" I asked. The aged face sunk back below the bark without a word. Nonplussed, I returned to my original task.

I took off my tie, and unbuttoned my shirt. I soaked the shirt in the stream, and it held water, but for how long? I decided to take off my pants and soak them as well. I kept the pockets dry so that my wallet and lighter would not get wet. The pants soaked up much more water than the shirt. Shirtless, I restrung the tie around my neck. No one can say I don't have a sense of style. I started up the hill. I was wearing only a tie, boxers, and shoes.

Again, the hill was my enemy. The hike was now familiar to me. The turns and views were no new surprise. I knew what lay ahead. The hill sapped at my strength, and again I became thirsty. The clothes were not dripping any more. I agonized over whether to squeeze some of the water into my own mouth. The desire rose strongly in me. It was like being in a candy shop without having a single penny to buy candy. But, it was more than this, because what were holding me back were my own conflicting desires. I held out against the impulse to drink and climbed the hill with renewed vigor. I reached the ridge and made my way to the clearing.

The wolf was eyeing me as soon as I came to the end of the trail. He had not moved at all from his spot. The clothes were still wet enough for a good drink, it seemed, but I was nervous about approaching the wolf. I approached him carefully, but he made no sudden moves. I started with the shirt first. The wolf lifted his head as I squeezed the shirt above his mouth. A thin stream of water came out. The water mostly wet his tongue as he tried to swallow some of it. I wrung the shirt totally out of any water I could force from it. Then, I started on the pants. One leg at a time, I tried to get water into the wolf's mouth. The water was harder to get out of the pants, but there was more of it. After the pants were finished, the wolf lay his head back on the ground with a sigh.

There was nothing for it now but to look at the leg. As I started to examine it, I again felt the sense of being watched. Out of the corner of my eye, I saw the old man's face in the tree again. It spoke. "Value of life is highly regarded. To help with the bleeding, there is a leaf from a bush with white flowers on the ridge." The face watched over me again. I remembered the bush from the trail, and went back to get some. I stripped several branches of their leaves. I brought the leaves back to the wolf. The face was still present, watching. It seemed always to be aware.

I examined the leg of the wolf without touching it. I knew nothing of medicine, but it was obvious that a splint of some sort was necessary. It appeared that the bone could just be pulled straight back into place. I was sure this would be an extremely painful process, and I wasn't sure how the wolf would react. "This is going to hurt, wolf, but I have to do it. Your leg needs to be fixed as best as I can and I'm the only one that can do it." I found two straight sticks and ripped some strips from my shirt. I approached the wolf carefully. His eyes never left mine, but he did not threaten me. So, I gingerly felt the broken leg. The bone stuck partway through the skin and was broken roughly diagonally. I pulled straight down from the paw and felt the bone slide back beneath the flesh. The wolf growled loudly. I had no idea whether the bone was in place or not, but it didn't seem too bumpy at the break, so I decided to apply the leaves and splint. I crushed some of the leaves between my hands. I put the crushed leaves about the wound, and tied one of the strips of my shirt around it. Then, I put the straight sticks on either side of the break, and tied them together tightly. The wolf growled again at this treatment. I consoled him. "It looks much better now, Wolf, believe me."

The wolf spoke again. "Never be the same."

I sighed sadly. "No, probably not. I'm not any

29

kind of doctor."

The wolf lay his head back on the ground for a moment. Then, surprisingly, he heaved himself up on three legs. He spoke. "More water."

I was shocked. "Are you able to walk?"

The wolf looked at me under his heavy brows. "Pain is only to let you know." We decided to try to make the trek back again to where the stream lay, my fourth time hiking the trail. The wolf avoided touching his hurt leg to the ground at all. He followed me with an ungainly gait, but I did not need to slow down much. We made it to the stream without incident, and the wolf lapped thirstily at the water. Soon, our sometime friend, the old man in the tree appeared.

I accosted him. "I hope those leaves aren't poison or something. I put them right on the wound."

The tree man responded. "That is as it should be." The wolf looked back around and growled.

I looked at the wolf in surprise. "You know this old face in the tree?" The wolf nodded his head and growled again. I asked the wolf about this. "How do you know him? Did he hurt you somehow?"

The wolf hung his head a little and answered. "He would not show me the way out of this enchanted forest. I kept running after him. The face just moved from tree to tree. Then, on top of the mountain, I broke my leg on a stone." It was more than the wolf had ever said before, and he said it in a halting, broken way.

I turned to the face. "How about it, old man? Will you show us the way out of the forest?"

The face in the tree responded. "The forest cries for

justice. Reap only what you sow."

I narrowed my eyes a little. "No, that's not really answering the question. We need a way out of the forest."

"Every tree in the forest is one. I am the advocate of that spirit."

"OK, OK," I said, "Now we're getting somewhere. In what way do you represent the forest?" The wolf paid more attention to the conversation as the tree responded.

"The forest heals all ills and centers you to yourself."

I shook my head again. "No, no, -You, what sort of spirit are you?"

The forest spirit hesitated for a moment. "I guide, I protect, I inform."

I pleaded with the spirit. "So please guide us out of the forest. We are lost and hungry." The wolf growled in agreement.

The spirit spoke more quickly, as if on safer ground. "The forest reaches calmly in two directions."

I thought on that one for a minute, and then I thought about the whole conversation. "What happens if I just say the word 'forest'?" I asked.

The spirit responded. "The forest lives in circles."

I chuckled a little, and spoke to the wolf. "You see how this is going, don't you?" The wolf nodded but did not speak. I turned my attention back to the tree spirit. "We want to go home. We are looking for our home."

The tree spirit hesitated again. "Home is where you make it. The forest is one spirit."

"Yes, but we want the path to home. There should be a path out." I was determined not to say the word 'forest.'

"The true path lies in respecting the one spirit of the forest." I was starting to get a little desperate now.

"We promise to respect the forest in all we do, but we cannot survive here in the forest by ourselves. Show us the path to our home, and we will continue to respect the forest." I said 'forest' a bunch of times in that statement, but I was hoping for the best.

This time, the forest spirit acquiesced. "The path lies along the creek, as it always has. Respect the forest." The forest spirit sunk back beneath the bark, effectively ending the conversation. I looked up and down the path by the creek. In fact, there was a down way, through the brambles. I had not seen it before. I decided to get a drink of water and continue downstream on the path near the brambles.

Wolf and I made our way along the creek. It was fairly easy going. The birds were singing all of their different songs, which I hadn't noticed before. After only a few miles, the path brought us to the back yards of a row of houses. It was a welcome sight, but there was an iron fence enclosing the area. The top of the fence was spiked, so it did not look easy to climb over. No people were in their back yards, so we continued along the path.

Eventually, we came to a junction between two communities. There were two ways to tell this. First, there was an identical fence running perpendicular to the back yard fence. Second, the houses changed architecturally. The new group had a similar look, but now different from the previous houses. The path kept going behind the houses, so we kept on as well. No one was in sight.

We passed three more communities, all close to

identical, before we could make a right turn around the fence. We made the right turn, and there was a field opening out to our left. The fence continued on our right, and we were still looking at the back yards of houses that no one used. Maybe it wasn't the right time of day. But hopefully, we would now make it to the front of the housing community. Darkness was beginning to fall. It was my second day without food. Wolf was not complaining, but then, he was not speaking at all. Fortunately, after we passed ten similar houses, the fence took a right again, and we were at the front of the community. The fence continued to an entrance that was gated, and we stood there gazing at it.

"I say we try to get in and beg some food," I said. I had some money left in my wallet, so we could buy it if necessary. Wolf said nothing. We had seen no one moving, and the road that led up to the gate looked as if it might be a long one. We waited outside the gate, looking in. The windows of the houses lit up, almost at the same time. It was strange. The windows had bars on them, similar in style to the fences around the community. No people could be seen through the windows.

A car pulled up to the gate. It was an expensive luxury car, and the driver was the only one in it. I waved and shouted, but the car stopped only to let the gate swing open. The driver never looked at me. When the car passed through the gate, it started to swing shut. Wolf and I ran through the gate just before it closed. I was back in civilization, with a new friend by my side.

❖ Chapter 3

"The very essence of a free government consists in considering offices as public trusts, bestowed for the good of the country, and not for the benefit of an individual or a party."
John C. Calhoun, Speech

Wolf and I walked up to the first house on the corner. The lights were on, so we assumed that someone was home. I rang the doorbell and waited. No one came to the door. I rang it again, and still no one answered. We moved to the next house. Again, the doorbell brought no response. "That's strange," I said to Wolf, "There seems to be no one here." We rang doorbells at all the houses along the outside of the community, and no one answered at all. It was now quite dark.

We knew at least one person was here, so we didn't worry too much, but we were still very hungry. Finally we rang a doorbell, and the man who had driven past us answered. "Hello? What can I do for you?"

I spoke up right away. "Oh, I'm so glad you answered. We have traveled a long way, and we have not eaten or had anything to drink in a long while. Would you be so kind as to give us or sell us some food?"

He looked at Wolf for the first time. "Hey, we don't allow... dogs here," he said. "That dog has to go."

I looked at Wolf for a second. "My dog won't hurt anyone, he's absolutely tame." Wolf looked anything but tame and growled loudly.

The man didn't seem to hear. He paused and made a decision. "Well, I guess I could give you some food, but you'll have to stay out there."

I was ecstatic. "That's wonderful, we would be so grateful." The man closed the door. We waited outside for about ten minutes on the stoop. He reappeared with some ham and cheese sandwiches and a glass of orange juice. I asked him for a pan of water for Wolf, and he brought one. We tore into the food, in different ways. I ate a sandwich like a normal person, and Wolf spread his out all over the yard. He seemed to have trouble eating anything except the ham.

The man had watched us eat our food for awhile, but now he wanted to go back inside. "Just make your way along, now. I don't want any trouble from you."

I stopped eating and said, "Thank you very much, we will. Hey, which way is ------? How far is it?"

The man looked confused. "------? I've never heard of it. The nearest town is Iffil. It's about fifteen miles down the road to the right."

I was concerned but not overly surprised. "Okay, we'll head in that direction. Thanks again for all your help." The man turned his back and shut the door. We finished up our food and left. The stars were out, and all of the houses were venting smoke out of their chimneys. I looked back at the house one time, and I saw a small shadowy figure from the upstairs window. It appeared the figure was on the phone and calling someone while looking at us from a darkened frame.

We walked to the front gate of the housing community, and there was a push button to open it from the inside. No such amenity existed outside, and I suppose that the gate would be made pointless if there was a button

35

to open it from the outside. I looked at Wolf. "I think you should stay with me. There's no way you could catch your food right now. Your leg is too poor. Why don't we walk as far as we can towards town and then sleep somewhere by the side of the road?" Wolf did not say anything but did not leave my side either. We walked along the road for awhile, passing the gated communities we had passed before. No cars passed us at this time of the night, though it was not really all that late.

We walked on for a few miles, when I saw headlights off in the far distance coming our way. I had a funny feeling and did not want to be seen. I decided to leave the road and hide in the trees. Wolf followed me. We watched as three identical white vans zoomed past our position, certainly speeding. There were no windows to show what might be carried in the back of these vans. The vans quickly disappeared from view. Wolf growled and lay down.

"This seems to be as good a place as any to stop," I said, "I'm tired anyway." I lay down with my back to Wolf's and tried to get comfortable. It's never easy when you're lying on the ground, but the sound of crickets eventually lulled me to sleep. As I slept, I dreamed.

I was in a room that held mostly darkness. The only light came from a window on the far side of the room. For some reason, I was drawn to the window. It was an effort to get to the window, but I worked and came closer. I could see the Venetian blinds. Then, as I reached the window, I stooped and picked something up and threw it through the window. It went through without disturbing anything, but I felt like I was throwing a tiny hand grenade. Suddenly I was free in space. A great fiery eye was inspecting me. The pupil dilated and contracted. Then, consciousnesses gathered around me and flung themselves in the shape of a snake at the eye. The eye dissolved and lost color. The snake of minds threw itself forward, like a rushing train. The eye tried to reform to block it, but it was pale and colorless. It could not completely form. Suddenly, I protested. "Hey, this isn't nice!" The snake of minds hesitated for a split instant, but then continued on. I found myself somewhere else.

I was sick and in bed. I seemed near death's door. I was a woman! That didn't seem to bother me. There was a beautiful blond woman near me, and one of my other friends there. The male in me reached out, attracted to the woman, but I could not move. The woman didn't think that I could see or hear, I guess. She pulled something from my purse. "I've got her credit card! Let's go." They left happily. A great sadness overwhelmed me. I had a cash bill of impossibly large denomination in my hands. I folded it and let it fall to the floor. Had it been for the beautiful blond woman? I don't know. My husband appeared, yelling at me. He seemed of Middle Eastern descent, and I couldn't understand his words. Mostly he was angry that I was wasting money. But the money had been mine! I found myself somewhere else.

I was in a bathroom in a familiar house. I could not see anything, but I sensed everything around me. For some reason my body was exhausted, but my mind was alert. There was a pipe and a lighter on the counter next to me. I quickly slipped it into my pocket and tried to crawl out of the bathroom. I had barely made it into the hallway, when I collapsed to the floor, unable to go any farther. Suddenly, some people surrounded me, a man and some very young children. They moved about, seemingly very busy. The man leaned over to me. "Are you alright to drive home?" I nodded yes, as one will always do. I could not even get off the floor. The children came and hugged me one at a time. Each of them gave me a feeling of love and energy. Then the dream changed for the worse.

Another man kicked in the door of the house. He was an evil man, you could just sense it. He had children of his own surrounding him. They didn't seem evil, but just tied to him body and soul. The whole group of people left me in the hallway and went into another part of the house. They conversed for awhile, but I could not hear what was said. The evil man seemed to have a measure of authority over the nicer man. Then I heard the nicer man say in a hesitating manner, "I'll go outside with you." The group returned to the hallway, and the evil man kicked me in the back on the way out. The nicer man laid his hand on my head briefly and tousled my hair. The two men and all the children went outside. I lay in the hallway, still exhausted. I lay there waiting for something to happen, when I realized I could see the early light of day. I was not lying in a familiar house; I was lying next to Wolf in the forest by the side of a road.

Wolf awakened when I did, and struggled to his feet. The broken leg was still tormenting him. I stood and took a look at it. The splint had come loose from all of the walking we were doing, even though he was not putting any weight on the leg. I carefully tied the splint together again. At least the bleeding had stopped, and the flesh was mostly pushed together. It seemed to be healing. As I examined the wound, we heard the sound of vehicles on the road again. We were pretty far into the woods, but we could see two white vans passing slowly down the road. This time we could see someone searching the trees with binoculars from the passenger seat. The remains of my red shirt must have stood out, so I crouched behind a tree.

"Do you think they're looking for us?" I asked Wolf. He growled in reply and stood near me. The vans passed on. We waited for what seemed like fifteen minutes in the woods, but it was probably only ten. Then we went back to the road. "Why would anyone be looking for us?" I mused to myself. We hiked along the way to Iffil. It wasn't long before we encountered normal traffic, mostly headed the way we were going. I hoped none of the white vans would travel this way. We started to pass houses and small stores. I saw a small clothing store. I looked down at my tattered shirt and decided to enter. Wolf came inside with me.

There were men's shirts and pants on different sides of the store. It was a men's store so there was no women's clothing, but there seemed to be more women in the store than men. I had a good amount of cash on me, so I felt I could get a nice shirt. I looked at striped green ones and plaid red ones. I don't like any pattern to be too bold, but it seems hard not to get something like that. I finally settled on a light blue shirt that had large white outlines of squares. Almost anything goes with black pants. I tried it on in the dressing rooms, as Wolf paced around outside. It was a good fit. You should always take the time to try on your clothes before you buy them. I wore the shirt out to the sales counter. The salesman took off the security tag and rang it up. He was even nice enough to clip off the labels for me. I gave him my old red shirt so he could dispose of it.

"This is distressed nicely," he joked, "We may sell this for double what you paid for your shirt." It was nice of him to try to make a connection with me when it was not really necessary.

I looked down at Wolf. "Say goodbye to the nice man, Wolf." Wolf inclined his head but did not say anything.

The man looked at me a little strangely. "Yes, goodbye." Wolf and I left the store. We walked again down the road. As we passed more houses and stores, I assumed we had entered the city limits of Iffil proper. However, this proved not to be the case. As we walked along, we saw ahead of us a great wall. It was made of stone and had towers at the corners. There was a great gate that the road passed through. Cars moved through without challenge. There seemed to be no real way in for pedestrians other than squeezing by along with the cars. This is what we did to enter the town.

We managed to get inside town without being hit. Once we passed the gate, there were sidewalks. Tall buildings lined the streets. There were stores and cafes all along the way. I saw a clothing store with red awnings over its doors and windows. Several small carts occupied available space, selling specialty foods. There was a pawnshop with wares on display: watches, jewelry, musical instruments. Some of these instruments were of a design I had never seen before. There was one guitar-like instrument that had two necks in a "V." One of the necks had bass strings and one of the necks had guitar strings. Both sets of strings passed over a large sound hole. I was curious how much something like that might cost, but there's no real purpose in asking when you know you're not going to buy.

Wolf and I wandered on. The pedestrian traffic seemed to be getting stronger toward the center of town so we walked in that direction. As we walked, people glanced at Wolf in passing. He seemed to provoke reaction like a confessional would. The people without guilt did not fear him. Some were clearly frightened. Then, we passed a man who was playing violin on the street corner. His case was open, and there was a decent amount of money in it. He winked as he played and said, "That's a beautiful animal you've got there." I nodded and walked past as he played a special run of notes for us. Something made me glance behind me as I walked. Far away behind us, I saw a bald man stepping out of a white van. His eyes were the strangest thing. They seemed to shine with a cloudy red fire that smoked into the air. He pointed in our direction, and men dressed in black erupted from the back of the van and ran toward us. In response, I took off towards the center of town, weaving between people. Wolf ran ahead of me, having no problem keeping up the pace despite his healing leg. Luckily, the crowd thickened as we reached a large park. There seemed to be a festival going on. Clowns walked on stilts. Jugglers threw balls into the air. There was a large stage in the distance with familiar music playing. We ducked behind a food vendor, and we could see the disturbance as the men in black fought their way through the crowd. Wolf growled softly, but he seemed to see the need for discretion. We waited there a long while, until we thought that the coast was clear.

As I bought some hot dogs from the food vendor, I realized that the music we were listening to was none other than The Dugouts. There were a crazy number of people between us and the stage, all dancing happily. I was determined to investigate this, the only link between my own world, and the strange world I found myself in. We made our way closer to the stage. At first, people blocked us by not getting out of our way. They seemed annoyed at our passage. Then, the music started to build, and we were ignored. The music rose in volume and pitch, and the crowd grew more frenzied. The singer started to swing his ropy braids around his head. We inched up closer until we were between the sound booth and the stage. We could get no closer. Astonishingly, the singer's beaded braids had lengthened. They now weaved about the whole stage in time to the music. They were thick and numerous, too numerous to all be coming from the singer's head, and yet it seemed to be.

The pitch of the music was rising impossibly, and then with a crash of the cymbals, the braids shot out into the crowd. People started grabbing on to the lengths of beaded hair. A fat bearded man near us got one and hung on for dear life. As many braids as there were, the crowd was yet larger, and scuffles broke out to see who could get to a braid. There was a disturbance at the back of the crowd. Armies of men in black had been deposited on the edge of the grounds, and they struggled forward toward the stage. The bass player started a slow powerful groove, and an amazing thing happened.

The stage started to detach itself from the ground and lift into the sky. The guitar player mirrored the groove of the bass player, and the stage ascended faster. Slowly, the braids pulled taut. The singer screamed as if he was giving birth, or perhaps more aptly, as if all the hair on his head were being pulled out. People were dragged towards the stage as it lifted higher. I looked back over my shoulder and noticed the men in black drawing closer. At that point, a long braid swung near us. It was flying in the air already, and I had to jump to reach it. I held on with my hands, and wrapped my feet around it when I could. Wolf ran around uncertainly, unable to reach it.

I yelled to him. "Get to a braid, Wolf!" He howled and ran around some more, but then a braid came near to him. He jumped in the air and caught it with his teeth. Both of us were lifted into the air beneath the stage. The music continued to play as the singer screamed.

Higher and higher we went. The bearded fat man swung by and smiled. His tooth was missing, and it seemed an incongruous moment. An attractive girl in a skirt swung by above us. It was hard not to look up her skirt as she kicked her legs around, but I managed to be a gentleman about it. Soon we were passing through the clouds. The stage rose above them and brought all the people higher than the clouds. Then it started to descend. As each individual touched down on the cloud's surface, they were buoyed up. Wolf landed on the cloud before I did, but I landed safely as well. The cloud was slippery, but stable. There were fluffy pockets you could lie in. As people relaxed their grip on the singer's hair, his screams lowered in volume. Eventually, the stage landed on one side of the cloud, and you could see the singer panting with his head down. The band continued to play a soft melody, appropriate to the situation. About a hundred of us climbed our way closer to the stage, applauding for some reason. The Dugouts nodded and stopped.

I was still determined to find out how to get back to my own world. People crowded the stage, hands outstretched to touch the band. The Dugouts put down their instruments and jumped into the crowd. They were tossed around for awhile, but eventually let down to the cloud's surface. People pounded their backs and shook their hands. Wolf and I made our way to the singer.

His braids looked normal size again, and he stood drinking a bottled water. Wolf went up and sniffed around his crotch. This was the first time he had done anything so rude, but the singer didn't seem to mind.

The singer looked down at Wolf. "Nothing there you need to know about, Wolfman."

I walked up to him as Wolf sat down. "You guys are fantastic, really!" I said. "Beautiful things happen when you play."

The singer nodded. "Yes, it's a great responsibility. We try to take it seriously."

I continued earnestly. "Last time I saw you guys, I was in ------. Then, I somehow found myself in a forest world. Now, I'm in the clouds. How am I to get back to my own world?"

The singer nodded sadly. "Yes, well, we travel a lot. The way is hard and dangerous. We usually get back to where we've started from, but it can take awhile. Home is not ever the same when we get back. If you leave somewhere, it's not the same when you return."

"Will you take us with you?" I asked. "I want to get all the way back to my home."

The singer looked at me carefully. "Of course," he said, "What did you think we were going to do, leave you in the clouds? However, I do not take responsibility for your actions. You do what you want, but don't come crying to me if it doesn't work out the way you want it to."

I could sense that he was preparing to turn his attention elsewhere, and I tried to engage him. "Tell me more of these worlds we are in. There seem to be people after me."

He started to turn away. "Come to the front of the stage in an hour; we'll talk with some of the newer fans." Then, he walked off aimlessly into the crowd. Some people came up to Wolf and me after the singer walked away. The bearded fat man was there, and he chimed in first.

"What did Robbins have to say to you? Is he as cool in person as he is on stage?"

I did not really know how to answer. "Well, I guess so. We talked about finding my way home."

A pale man with black hair and studded leather clothes laughed. "Home?! I'm along for the ride now! They hooked us up!" The small crowd around me laughed with him.

A short girl with red hair spoke next. "We're just getting started, don't you see? I don't think you know what you're in for." Wolf growled as the crowd pressed too close.

The gap-toothed bearded man jumped back. "Hey, is that wolf tame? He seems kind of angry."

I smiled inwardly at the one advantage that I had

over these people. "Oh, I don't know if he's tame or not. We just started traveling together not too long ago. In fact, I think he wants some time by himself." The crowd respected my wishes and dispersed except for the small redhead. She looked at Wolf closely and approached him.

"Hey big wolf," she said, praising him. "You're a fine specimen." Wolf easily out-massed her by a couple a hundred pounds. She put her hand out and let him sniff it. Then she scratched his ears. "You're not so fierce, are you?" Wolf sat down and let her scratch his head. I looked around the cloud as it shifted and flew with the wind. It was a wild feeling not ever having a firm footing, but always sliding.

"You seem to have a way with animals," I said.

"Yes, I always have. My name is Kirsten. What's his name?" She said, looking at Wolf.

"Well, I call him Wolf, and he doesn't seem to mind."

Wolf actually spoke up for the first time in ages. "My real name is Growl at the Moon, but as there are no other wolves around, Wolf will do nicely."

Kirsten looked shocked. "He speaks! Amazing! Like the Wolf of legend."

I was puzzled. "Like what Wolf of legend?" I asked.

"It's a long tale," she said, "and an old one. Would you care to hear it?"

"Yes, I believe I would," I said. "Let's get more comfortable and lie down in the hollows of these clouds." That was exactly what we did, and she began to tell the tale.

Chapter 4

"Happiness depends, as Nature shows, less on exterior things than most suppose."
William Cowper, Table Talk

"Once, there were no small towns, or individual houses," Kirsten began. "Everyone lived in a stronghold called a 'Folden.' The farmers had to work the fields under guard, and cattle were kept within the city walls. The fear for our safety was caused by an evil army. They were called The Black Borzhat, and they were comprised of many different evil beings. The Black Borzhat terrorized the Folden, building engines to breach the walls and gates. They tortured anyone they could catch for information on movements of the people. Then they would sacrifice the captives in a ceremony that would spill their blood into a special kind of crystal.

"These crystals were the heart and soul of the Borzhat. The Borzhat could communicate with each other through them. They also drew their strength from the crystal. The closer they were to the crystal, the stronger they became. Often, the Borzhat would bring one or more crystals to a siege of a Folden. They would gather strength from the proximity of the crystals and fight like demons.

"Once, during a siege of a particularly large stronghold called Ariphere, a crystal was captured. It happened this way. A sortie of knights burst through the gates of Ariphere during the thick of the battle and fought their way to an encampment of the Borzhat. The Borzhat had been scaling the walls of the city, and most of their army was away from the encampment. The evil priests of the Borzhat were there, men whose eyes leaked fire. They tried to sway the minds of the sortie with fear, but the men of the Folden were determined. They slew the priests and tried to break the crystal to destroy the power of the Borzhat, but they could not. As the Borzhat army began to realize what had happened, they became even more frenzied. They abandoned the ladders on the walls and started to run back to the encampment. The sortie had to take the crystal back with them and fight their way back to Ariphere. Many of them died, but the gates opened, and the crystal made it safely back within the walls of the town.

"At first, the Borzhat attacked the town with a ferocity never before seen. They seemed disorganized, attacking here and there without plan. The city was succeeding in repelling them. While the battle was going on, the town elders discussed what to do with the crystal. They knew of no way to use it, and they knew also that the Borzhat relied heavily on its powers. The town elders decided to take the crystal to a smith and ask him to break it. The smith used heat and hammer and anvil. He used edged weapons and crushing devices. None would break the crystal.

"Then the attacks subsided, and the Borzhat seemed to just be waiting outside the gates. They massed in large numbers so that no one could exit the gates again. More armies arrived at Ariphere. They camped at each of the points of the compass around the Folden. One night, glowing, twisting smoke began to rise from the camps of the enemy. The smoke was different colors, as the crystals were different colors. Within the columns of smoke, high above the camps, a giant pair of eyes could be seen. The eyes were focused on the city of Ariphere. They looked through the walls toward a point within the city. Not a person in the city was unaware of where the eyes were staring. The town elders became more agitated, arguing about what was to be done with the crystal. With their indecision lay their demise. The smith valiantly continued to try to break the crystal. The oldest town elder argued that the crystal should be thrown over the walls back to the Borzhat. However, this was the first time a crystal had ever been captured, and the others were still hopeful.

"As the smith hammered away, a red smoke began to issue from the red crystal. The smoke poured out, and as the people breathed it in they began to choke. It filled their lungs with poison, and they died slowly. The smith used his last strength to put the crystal in a bucket of water, but the smoke boiled out of the water anyway. It poured out of the windows of the building, and the people near began to choke and die. As it became obvious what was happening, the whole of the city tried to fight their way out. The knights of the city led the way, and the townspeople followed with farming implements and knives. But the Borzhat were ready, and they slaughtered all but a few that escaped to the forest." Kirsten stopped and scooped up a bit of cloud in her hand. She stuffed it into her mouth and swallowed. I had not thought to do that, but I was thirsty, so I did the same. Wolf gnawed off a piece and licked his chops.

She continued. "The other Folden learned about this through word of mouth and concern grew. One of their only hopes had been to capture the crystals and destroy them, and now it seemed that this was impossible. A council of the wisest elders from different strongholds decided to meet to discuss the problem. They met secretly at a small stronghold in the center of the realm, a Folden called Yverryten. Historically, The Black Borzhat had been nothing but raiders, stealing and killing here and there. Over time, they grew and strengthened until the cities had to be surrounded with walls. Now they destroyed whole cities with their might.

"Most of the elders argued for the creation of an alliance army, made up of knights from many different cities. Some elders urged caution at this, saying the Borzhat disappeared into the mountains that were perfect for ambushes and rockslides. If the alliance army were defeated, there would be no one to protect the Folden. The elders that lived by the sea had mighty ships that were never used in the battles. They counseled building enough ships to sail across the ocean to other lands. Secretly, they believed that if things got much worse, they would sail their own people away anyway. The elders that lived closest to the mountains asked for help from the stronger cities, saying they could defeat the Borzhat and keep them bottled up in the mountains.

"Unfortunately, as the council went on for days and days, the city was encircled by a Borzhat army. Truly, the Borzhat did not know that the most important people of the realm were there, or they would have brought a larger force. They had two crystals, one for each gate, and they brought numerous henchmen. The bulk of the Borzhat were goblins of a sort. They were short and thin, with pale warty skin. Their heads were mostly bald, and they had pointed ears. Their arms were long, reaching almost to the ground, and they carried knives or clubs. They wore no armor, but their skin was leathery and thick. These Borzhat were not hard to kill, but they were numerous, so there were always four or five attacking a single knight. More rare were the trolls. These Borzhat had grossly fat bellies, so that they leaned back when they walked. The trolls were seven or eight feet tall, and they also had long arms. They were often the ones that would try to break the gates of the cities. Both of these Borzhat were stupid creatures, relying only on their strength. Their masters were the priests. These priests were humanlike in appearance, but their eyes leaked colored fire, the same color as the crystals they worshipped. The priests would control the other Borzhat with their minds, and could induce emotion in almost anyone. Fear and hatred were their strongest weapons. There were other beasts that were ridden, and evil pets that were bred in the mountains, but these three types of Borzhat comprised the bulk of the armies.

"Yverryten was surrounded, but each of the elders had brought a sizeable force with them to protect themselves. The battle was fierce, but the knights of Yverryten prevailed, and they managed to capture both crystals that had been brought to the siege. They had to kill every last Borzhat to do this, as the Borzhat fought to the last to defend the crystals. Now the elders had a new subject to debate. What were they to do with the crystals? Some argued that they should be buried deeply. Some argued that they should be thrown into the sea. Others argued that there might still be a way to destroy them that had not been tried yet. While they argued, a pair of heroes emerged onto the scene.

"They came from the forest, an old bearded man with a staff and a wolf the size of a small bear." Kirsten stopped and looked at Wolf significantly. "The man and the wolf went up to the city gates and demanded to see the elders. The soldiers at the gate let them in, but did not want to notify the elders of their presence, as the elders were deep in council.

"Then the wolf spoke. 'We have observed the battle from the forest. I even killed a few Borzhat scouts. You must let us investigate the crystals.' The soldiers were surprised, as they had never heard a wolf speak before. They decided to send a messenger to the council to see if they wanted to speak to the old man and the wolf. In this case, the council was wise, for they had not decided anything else. They let the pair into the council room. The old man walked to the long table where the crystals were lying.

" 'The crystals are a matter of mind. Destroying them is not so much a matter of force, as it is a matter of force of will.' He concentrated, and then touched his staff to the green crystal. The crystal shattered on the table, and the pieces evaporated like water on a hot skillet. He concentrated again, and touched his staff to the red crystal. Again, the crystal shattered and evaporated. The elders were ecstatic. Finally, they had a course of action. They could fight, and capture the crystals and destroy them. They begged the old man and the wolf to travel with them to the cities that had the best defenses. The old man would travel with an army, and destroy the crystals when they were captured. The old man readily agreed. He had been a hermit, and a forest walker, and the Borzhat were not kind to trees.

"The elders retired to their respective cities, and the old man and the wolf were brought to one of the strongest Folden. The old man was taught to ride a horse, and a traveling army was created. The bravest knights and lancers were chosen to travel to the places where the Borzhat were attacking. The Folden would send a messenger to this army when they were under attack, and the army would respond. In the first battle, they were used to aid a small city near the mountains. The city was besieged, but the rescuing army was able to sneak up on the Borzhat. The lancers charged and destroyed the priests, and the old man hurried into the encampment. The wolf prowled around him looking for the enemy, but the knights had done a thorough job. The hermit destroyed the blue crystal with his staff, and an amazing thing happened. The Borzhat that were storming the walls seemed to lose all mobility. Their bones became jelly, and they fell to the ground like slugs. The city rallied, and killed the Borzhat where they lay. There was another crystal and army, but now it was outmatched. The lancers circled around and attacked the other encampment. This time the Borzhat had fallen back to the crystal, and they fought hysterically, but they were pressed on all sides by the liberating army and the city guards. The wolf drove into the encampment and tore out the throat of the chief priest while the battle was still raging. Then he turned and grabbed the crystal in his teeth and ran back to the old man. The Borzhat chased after him, but the old man destroyed the crystal, and again they fell to the ground.

"This was the end of the first battle, and there was celebration in the Folden that night. However, the war was not over. After several succeeding losses, the Borzhat began to group in larger numbers, becoming more difficult to attack. The new victories prompted alliances between the Folden, and larger armies were sent to combat them. After years of struggle, the Borzhat were mostly defeated, and retreated to the mountains. All through these battles, the old man went from place to place, destroying crystals. He contended that anyone could do it, but though many tried, no one ever succeeded. The powers of his staff grew to legend. He was even older now and tired of fighting. He only wished to return to the forest and live simply with the wolf.

"The city elders persuaded him to take the battle to the mountains. There were still crystals out there, and the land was not yet liberated from the scourge of evil. The lancers were not able to bring their horses all the way into the mountains, so a foot company was assembled. The company marched into the mountains and flushed out many Borzhat from their caves. No crystals were found. Victory followed victory, and the company moved further into the mountains. Unfortunately, they were being led into an ambush. A rockslide destroyed the rear ranks of the company and bottled them in. Then the strongest of the Borzhat attacked them in force, overwhelming the men of the realm. The trolls issued in numbers never before seen from secret caves along the trail. They strove to reach the old man, who was protected in the center of the company. The company realized that they had to retreat at all costs, and they tried to climb over the landslide. A party of trolls fought their way to the old man and started killing his guards. The wolf leaped and savaged at the trolls, but there were too many. The wolf was killed first, and then the old man. One of the soldiers grabbed the old man's staff and fled with the surviving members of the company. The bedraggled crew reached their base camp, and news quickly spread of their defeat.

"The Folden were enraged and distraught about the loss of the old man. Many were available for a return to the mountains, but the elders urged caution. They feared the magic of the last crystals and wished to leave the remnant of the Borzhat army alone. The elders took the staff of legend and hid it away from any possible threat. After this inconclusive battle in the mountains, there were no more attacks from the Borzhat. They faded into legend and myth."

Kirsten stopped and looked seriously at us. "The Borzhat priests have somehow insinuated their way into places of power again. Everyone knows the stories of their evil, yet no one stands up to the establishment that protects them. Their minions are no longer ugly monsters, but they are people just trying to survive. The Borzhat priests control what we buy, what we see, and where we go. It takes a great effort to fight them, but many realize that it must be done. The battle is joined by their actions, and waiting is no longer enough. These musicians, The Dugouts are a few that are taking the battle to many different places. We shall see where they take us this time. I believe it is time to gather at the front of the stage and see what they have to say."

Kirsten had talked for a long time, and she looked tired. I was entranced by her story. It was a history of a world I had never known. "Thank you for telling me your history," I said. "I am convinced that you feel strongly about your struggle against the Borzhat." We all stood up and made our way to the front of the stage. A crowd had already lined up at the front, and more people were arriving from different parts of the cloud. It appeared that almost everyone wanted to hear what Robbins had to say. Robbins walked on to the stage, and the small crowd applauded.

"Yeah, yeah. Whatever," he said. "Can you all hear me?" The crowd gave him a noncommittal answer, and he picked up a mike. "Okay, is this a little better? All right. Now all of you know there is an enemy, but not all of you know how to fight that enemy. It is not enough anymore just to fight them physically. We have to fight with principles. We have to fight with ideas. I shouldn't even be using the word fight. It is more important to gather and organize. Have a plan for the future, and the future will be ours. Ignorance is the enemy, and complacence is its weapon. Money is important, but local organization is even more important. We will never win a fight with money alone, because we are paying the enemy in everything we do. It is suspicious when things become more expensive, because the owners of industry will always be able to afford the expense. The ones who were already rich but do not control the industry will find their money worth less and less.

"As you may know, we travel between many different worlds trying to organize the resistance. You too can be a part of the grand design. In fact, unless you want to stay here on this cloud, you have to follow us. Once you make your decision, you're along for the ride until you decide to stop. If you decide to stop, it is highly unlikely

that you'll ever get a chance to go again. So the decision
you made in coming with us was not made lightly. You are
the chosen few. Now it's time to travel to a world like no
other. In this world, everyone sleeps. There is actually a
switch that will turn off your mind when you go to sleep.
Somehow, this switch has gotten stuck, and everyone sleeps
without dreaming. We are going to flip the switches and
wake up the people we feel are ready to be awake. Are there
any questions?"

The fat man with the gap between his teeth spoke
up. "What is this world called?"

Robbins answered, "It is called Earth. All worlds
are called Earth for some reason. Anybody else?"

I spoke up. "How is it that my money works on
this and other worlds when I came from a different world?"

Robbins answered again. "Money's the same
everywhere, man. It seems like you can't have enough of
it sometimes. Anybody else?" The crowd stirred but did
not answer. "Okay, are you ready for a show?" The crowd
cheered a little. "Come on, are you ready to go to another
world?" The crowd cheered more loudly. The rest of the
band walked onstage and picked up their instruments.
"I said are you ready for the music!" The crowd cheered
and applauded, and the drummer started hitting the snare
drum in beats of two. Then the bass slid down from a
high note and thumped a low rhythm. After the drummer
and the bass player joined together for awhile, the guitarist
echoed the bass in harmony. Robbins started to sing. He
sang of disenchantment and loss in a low voice. The crowd
swayed in time to the music. As the band played, the
cloud began to descend. The sky darkened quickly, but no

moon or stars came out. The cloud descended more, and we hovered over an unlit city. Robbins sang of freedom and dreams, and the cloud started to descend to a plaza. The city was built of skyscrapers. Some tapered to points, others were flat topped. No one could be seen, and there were no lights to show the way. The only light came from an ambient glow in the sky. The cloud was softly touching down, but there was a fountain in the middle of the plaza. It had a statue of a man on a horse in the middle of it. The statue started to poke through the middle of the cloud in front of the stage, and people had to shove each other to get out of the way. As the cloud fully landed, it dispersed. The cloud faded into wispy streamers, and people stumbled as they lit onto the plaza. The stage itself landed gently, with The Dugouts ending their song as it touched down.

Robbins spoke again. "You know the kind of people we need! We need to wake up dedicated, feeling, good people. Hopefully you'll be able to tell something about the people from their apartments. Stay in groups of four to eight, and you should do all right. Wake up some good people, but not everyone. They will be able to wake the right people once we've started. Now go! There is no time to lose."

❖ Chapter 5

"When wilt Thou save the people? O God of mercy, when? Not
kings and lords, but nations! Not thrones and crowns, but men!
Flowers of Thy heart, O God are they; Let them not pass, like weeds,
away- God save the people!"
Ebenezer Elliot, Corn Law Rhymes

Kirsten had stayed near to me during the descent, and she asked me if I wanted to start a group. I agreed, and we looked around for a couple of others. The bearded fat man seemed to be isolated from the forming groups so we asked him to join.

"I'll be glad to!" He said, "My name's Wiegly." We all gave our names except Wolf. I told Wiegly to call him Wolf. Everyone else seemed to be grouped up, so we were about to head out, when the bass player from The Dugouts ran up to us.

"Hey, Robbins wants me to keep an eye on you guys. He seems to think that wolf is something special." We all greeted him enthusiastically, as he was a link to our ticket away from this world. The city was dark and depressing. It weighed upon us like a heavy blanket. Steam issued from grates in the street. It was the breath of the city itself, hot and wet. We randomly chose an exit from the plaza and set off down the road. The bass player's name was Danno, and he seemed content to just follow us.

Kirsten spoke. "I think we should head down this road for awhile until we find a nicer looking neighborhood."

I responded. "Do you think any of it is going to look any less glum? I agree though, we need to get away from the other groups of people so we are waking people in a spread out area." We trudged down the street. Most of the tall buildings had dull entrances of glass. No lights could be seen. We passed block after block. Wiegly started to breathe a little more heavily. He seemed to be tiring quickly. We turned left at what seemed an opportune moment, then back to the right after a few blocks. The glass and concrete seemed endless. Then, after another left turn, we found a slight change in the buildings. The entrances were different. They had semicircular panes of glass above them. Or perhaps a flowery scrollwork. They were still dark and forbidding, but there seemed to be an effort to lighten the heavy stance of the building. We all decided to go into a building that had a stepped façade.

The entrance was not locked, and the elevator was working. We all piled into the elevator, and I pushed the fourth floor. The elevator rose, and we were silent. The door opened, and we exited into a dark hallway. This time, it was truly dark. It was hard to see each other, much less where we were going. Wolf led the way to a door as we felt our way down the hallway. The door was locked, but it was not very sturdy. Wiegly was happy to use his weight to break it open. The living room was a disappointment. It was richly furnished, but boring. There was a huge entertainment center centrally placed opposite the sofa, but no music or movies nearby. A small amount of light came in through the windows, but it was still very dark. Danno turned on the TV, but there was nothing but static on. Kirsten turned on a kitchen light. She inspected the refrigerator. There was nothing but microwave dinners in the freezer. There was no rotting food, no herbs and spices.

I spoke up at this point. "I say that we don't wake this guy up. He has no pictures on the walls, nothing but a huge TV in the living room. He's a nonentity."

Kirsten looked a little upset that she hadn't been the one to suggest it but she agreed with me completely. "Yes, it's true that he doesn't seem very creative. I think we need someone with more character to wake first." We trooped back out into the hallway and moved down the corridor. Wolf led the way again, and we stopped a few doors down. This time, the door was unlocked, and we walked into the living room of another apartment. Kirsten turned on a lamp that was near the door, and we looked around. The living room was studded with dead plants. Only a cactus by the window had survived. There was abstract art on the walls, colorful, but somehow not clashing. There was a big TV opposite the couch, but there was a profusion of movies that I'd never heard of there. There were titles like; "Her Ready Smile," "The Point," "Maybe yes, Maybe no," and "Kissing a Fool."

Danno spoke up. "The living room seems okay, how's the kitchen?"

Kirsten seemed to like checking out the kitchen, and she responded. "There's a beautiful handmade spice rack in here. I think it's cherry. The garbage can in here really stinks, even though it has a cover. I'm almost afraid to open the refrigerator. Plenty of food in the cupboards. Lots of cookware. I say we wake this guy up." Everyone seemed to agree, and we made our way single file into the bedroom. After we turned on the light in the bedroom, we found a girl with a crew cut sleeping soundly in front of us. Wiegly took some initiative, and started shaking her and

62

calling for her to wake.

Danno had to stop him. "No, Wiegmiester, there's a switch near the bed." It was on the night table. Danno looked it over. It looked like a countdown dial that had stopped counting down. He shrugged and turned the dial all the way to 0. The girl moaned and tossed and turned a little. Then, she cried out in pain, and her eyes opened.

She started, and then cried out in pain again. "Who… who are you people? My body feels like it's on fire."

I stepped forward. "You've been asleep for a long time," I said. "Practically your whole world is asleep right now. We're here to wake up whoever we can to get you back on your feet."

She looked amazed. "What are you trying to pull? Get out of my apartment now!"

I gestured to the dead plants in her bedroom. "Just look, the evidence is here. We mean you no harm."

She looked at the plants and a slow acceptance entered her eyes. "Let me get dressed, and maybe we can talk it over." We all left the bedroom so she could have some privacy. For the first time, we settled in the living room as if we were just companions. Wiegly and Kirsten sat on the couch. Danno took an easy chair, and I remained standing. I almost felt like saying, "Nice weather we're having," but I refrained. No one said anything.

After a few minutes, the girl with the crew cut came in, dressed in baggy sweats and tennis shoes. "My whole body hurts. I had to put on the loosest clothes I could find. Now what do you want from me?" We looked at each other.

Kirsten spoke up. "We want you to come with us and start waking people up. You'll be able to guide us to the good people of this land. We're not even from this world."

The girl with the crew cut looked skeptical. "That seems like a lot of responsibility. Our city was on the brink of a kind of war. A certain part of the populace was starting to own everything and marginalize everyone else. No one really did anything about it, though. How do you organize a resistance to something like that?"

Kirsten looked at her and smacked her palm on her fist. "This is our opportunity now! You can help us, I know you can."

Danno nodded and agreed with her. "Yes, anything that you can do would be helpful to the cause. Let's do what you think is right as soon as possible."

The girl with the crew cut thought a moment. "Well, there's a guy on the fourteenth floor that organizes parties sometimes. He seems to know a lot of good people, in this building and others. Let's go wake him up. But first, I've got to have something to eat. I'm absolutely starving."

We were hungry too, and we talked as Tina (the crew cut girl) made a big pot of canned soup. She ladled it out into bowls, and we ate the sausage and red beans. We talked about what to do about the ones that were still asleep.

Tina spoke out. "What are we supposed to do to the truly evil ones, just let them sleep? Or worse, kill them in their sleep? It's like we're running without a plan."

I tried to calm her down. "Let's take it one person at a time. If we wake the right people, then they can wake their friends, and those friends will wake others. Maybe it will be a popular movement." We all finished eating and decided to go up to Pete's place on fourteen.

The hallways were dark, but the buttons in the elevator lit up so we could see when we reached fourteen. This time, Tina led the way, and we followed her down the hallway. We went around a corner and came to a door like all the others. This time, the door was locked. There seemed to be extra locks on the door, and it took Wiegly several tries to break it down. He stumbled into the room, and we followed him carefully. The living room was a study in black leather furniture. There were candles on the shelves everywhere, and black lamps with dimmer switches. Some of the shelves had books with titles like; "Neverending Sorrow," "A Man and His Past," and "Wishing Well Kiss and Tell." Tina led the way into the bedroom where we all got a shock.   Pete was sitting up in his bed. He had long black hair and a pale face, and his eyes were open. "The bathwater always cools off eventually," he said, and then his head fell back onto the pillow. He thrashed around in the blankets that were already in disarray.

Tina spoke to him. "Pete, hey Pete, wake up, man!"

Danno looked thoughtful. "I think he's still asleep, he's just not sleeping easily." Tina turned the dial near the bed to 0, and Pete sat bolt upright in bed.

"How long have I been sleeping?" he asked.

I responded the best that I could. "It's been a long time, Pete. Almost everyone on this world is asleep. We believe that you can help us in our struggle against a terrible enemy." Pete threw aside his blankets and stood up. He was entirely nude. He walked to the glass porch door and looked out onto the darkened city. "I knew something was not right with the sleep machine. Perhaps it has saved us this time, though." Somehow, his pale skin had turned dark against the dim light of the window.

"What is that light over there?" he asked. We all joined him at the entrance to his porch. He threw open the door. Every gesture was a command, a power. He went out onto the porch, and we followed. His arm swept up, pointing to a distant part of the city. There was a flat building that was not very tall directly at the end of a street. All of its lights were on and blazing. Pete spoke again. "That is the jail for the most dangerous criminals of the city. That is the place reserved for murderers and rapists. I feel that something wrong is happening."

Somehow this man had made the small squabbles that Kirsten and I had had for leadership seem petty. Wolf growled loudly, and it turned into a howl into the night. Pete pushed his way back through us into his apartment. He put on some clothes, mostly black leather, of course.

Kirsten spoke up. "Shouldn't we tell the others? There's no telling what's going on at that jail."

Pete answered curtly. "There's no time. I'll wake up my friends down the hall, and we'll go." He clipped a knife to his belt and led the way into the hallway. "Tina, go get Alan in 1420. I'll get Ryan." The group walked back through the broken front door, and we split up. Wolf and I went with Pete, the rest with Tina. We decided to meet in the lobby. After everyone gathered in the lobby, we saw that the two men that Pete had woken were huge. Both were armed, one with a knife similar to Pete's, and Ryan had a gun. Pete commanded the room. Our group now numbered nine.

"We go to the federal jail!" Pete said. "Something is brewing there, and it's not right. We've slept long enough; the time to act is now!" We poured out into the street and started running in the direction of the jail. Pete and his friends led the way, as if they were breaking trail. Wolf had no trouble keeping up; his leg seemed to be healing fairly well, though he still didn't put any weight on it. Wiegly was the one that was lagging behind. Kirsten stayed with him, although she could clearly go faster. Somehow, the distance separating the first from the last never extended more than a city block, and we approached the jail. In the darkness of the city, it was the only lit up destination we could see. Pete, Alan, and Ryan reached the front door of the administrative portion of the jail. It was not locked. Ryan went through first, with his gun raised in the air, but no one was in the lobby. Alan held the door open as the rest of us filed through, Wiegly pulling up the rear. None of us had a real idea of where to go, but the layout of the place seemed to indicate that the deeper you went, the more secure it got. By intuition, we went deeper into the complex. We passed some rooms that were for visitors, where we could only access the public side of the room. We finally found a steel gate that led into the secure part of the facility. It was standing open. There was another gate just beyond it, and that was standing open as well. Ryan led the way again with his gun raised, and we followed tentatively. There was a feeling that, once through the gates, they might close behind us and leave us trapped.

We moved more slowly now, dreading a confrontation. Soon we came to the cells. They all stood open, but the inmates were asleep in their cells. But ahead, we heard a shouting, as if in triumph. We picked up the pace again, running down some stairs in the direction of the noise. At one row of cells, nasty-looking men wearing orange were darting in and out of cells. It was obvious what their motive was. They were waking up as many people they could as quickly as possible. Pete raised his hand to them and yelled. "Stop it now!"

The nearest of the inmates looked up and saw us. Then they ran at us insanely. Ryan stood with his gun pointed and waited until they were getting close, and then started firing. He took down four before they hesitated. The noise alerted the wing that something was going on. Fortunately, there weren't many inmates awake yet, and they didn't seem to have any weapons. They crowded in the walkway in front of us as Ryan faced them down. Pete and Alan both had their knives raised behind him. The rest of us watched as the inmates cursed and yelled.

Then there was a cry behind us. Wiegly was slumping to the floor with his head turned at a funny angle. There was an immense bald man with scars on his forehead behind Wiegly with his arms outstretched. Kirsten was closest to him. He dwarfed her. As she pressed back against Danno, the bald man reached for her. But Wolf growled and leapt. He went straight for the jugular. The man had his arms wide, and so could not protect his throat. Wolf over-bit however, and grabbed the sides of his neck. The man roared in pain, and his arms came together reflexively, hitting Wolf in the sides. Wolf started shaking his head back and forth, throwing the man off balance. The man fell backwards, with Wolf on top of him. That was the final straw, as Wolf's teeth ripped through an artery. There was another inmate behind us, but he was shorter and lean. Wolf growled at him, and the inmate backed off.

The inmates in front of us quieted down, and there was movement from the back of the crowd. They parted from the rear, and a man in black appeared. This man had a cloak of black with a high collar, and his eyes leaked green smoke. It trailed around his head as he walked forward. He ran a gloved hand over his black hair. As we had watched that incongruous move, his other hand had slipped into a belt pouch. Before we knew it, we were staring at a green crystal in his left hand. He smiled and raised the crystal.

"Shoot him!" Kirsten cried, but Ryan was unable to pull the trigger. It was as if time had stopped, and we were all stuck in place. The man with the green crystal sketched a line above his head. It stayed in the air like neon. He continued to sketch lines in the air, a vaguely rectangular shape. The final stroke was a line from the corner to the center. He paused. Then he punched the symbol with the crystal, and it exploded back at us. We covered our eyes with our arms and staggered. A window to another world appeared outlined in green, a world of colorful shapes and angles. Shouting could be heard from the other side of the window, and we could see the inmates rushing to it. The inmate from behind us tried to run past us to the window, but Pete grabbed him by the arm and threw him to the floor. Soon, the jail was silent, and we could peek around the side of the window and see that the inmates had left.

Soon, Kirsten was at Wiegly's side. She put a hand to the side of his neck but shook her head slowly.

"He's dead," she said, "that man must have broken

69

his neck."

Pete shook his captive and threatened him with the knife. "What do we do with you now? Where did they go to? What are they planning?"

The inmate looked confused. "We were promised freedom, that's all I know." A crafty look came into his eyes. "Let me go through, I'll never come back, I promise you."

Pete shook his head angrily in negation. "The world is better off without you littering it up. I could care less where the others went, but you're still our responsibility. Get in this cell here." He turned to Alan. "Alan, go find a way to close the doors to these cells. Ryan, keep this gate thing covered." Ryan reloaded and pointed his gun in the vicinity of the gate. After a time, an alarm sounded, and the doors to the cells slid shut. The inmate ran to the doors as if realizing his fate for the first time.

"No! Let me go free! I know more about the cloaked one. He knows the location of a magical staff. He was getting us to help him find and destroy it."

Pete sneered at him. "I care nothing of some magical staff. All I know is that we must protect this point of entry into our world. We're lucky it happens to be in a maximum security jail."

Kirsten jumped up, her red hair flying. "We must go after them! If that is the staff of legend, it can destroy the crystals and the Borzhat together."

Pete looked down at her. "No, I have no interest in following after escaped convicts. It's better that they are gone. I have much to do here on this sleeping world already."

She turned to Danno and pleaded with him. "Please, we must find the staff before they do, or at least keep them from destroying it."

Danno shook his head sadly. "No, my place is with the band. Separate, we can be broken, but together we make a powerful force. It's time I headed back." I could see where this was headed, and indecision washed over me. On the one hand, I knew that staying with the band was the easiest way to eventually find a way home. On the other hand, Kirsten had told me the whole history of her world, and showed me a compelling melodrama that was impossible to ignore. I felt on some level that the Borzhat would find their way to my world eventually. Perhaps they already had. Kirsten turned to me, and her eyes were glistening.

I answered before she had to ask. "I'll go, and I assume Wolf will come with me. Maybe something can be done, though I don't know what."

Kirsten smiled a little. "There's no time to lose. We must follow the Borzhat priest through the gate he has made." She looked around at Pete and the others from this dark world. "I wish you luck in your task of waking the world. Thank you for your help."

Pete nodded solemnly. "And thanks for yours," he said. "Because of you, this world has a chance now." Danno winked at us and said his goodbyes. He started away as Kirsten started for the green gate.

I stopped her quickly. "Maybe Wolf should go through first in case someone was left behind to guard the retreat." I said. Wolf growled at the thought and stepped up to the gate. He sniffed at it cautiously, and then jumped through. It was easy to see him pacing on the other world. It appeared that he stood on a flat red rectangle. Kirsten saw that he was all right and stepped through herself. I took a last look around at our comrades. Then I stepped through the gate with a sigh.

❖ Chapter 6

"If this is best of possible worlds, what then are the others?"
Francois M. A. Voltaire, Candide

I stepped through into a world of colors and shapes. Everything was a panel of different colors, and geometric oddities stuck out everywhere. It was easy to see our comrades back on the other world through the gate, but after a minute or so, they didn't pay any attention to us. Kirsten was looking at a yellow and orange pyramid on a square column. Wolf was sniffing around the gate. He eventually stood at one way down a red path.

"Is that the way they went, Wolf?" I asked him.

"Yes," he said. "They seemed to stay to the path." The path wound around small green cubes that were the size of stools. We decided to follow the path which was a series of red rectangles leading away through the solids around them. The green cubes clustered frequently for a while, as we made our way around a beige multi-faced mountain. Then the green cubes began to peter out in favor of yellow square columns. These branched out in a tree-like manner, and Kirsten held us up for a minute. She went among them and pulled on one of the smaller straight branches.

"If I can break one of these off, it might make a good staff," she said. She pulled hard at it, but it did not bend. She could feel the tension in it however, and continued. Suddenly, the branch broke off in her hands, with a sound like glass breaking. There was a keening sound among the yellow columns, and some of them changed their configuration. The branches twisted and locked into place. The place where the staff had broken off was a clean break. It was a lighter yellow color.

"Well, that did not go quite as I intended," said Kirsten. She looked mollified, but she had a good staff to walk with. We continued on down the red path. Wolf was still checking the trail for scent. He led the way. Uncharacteristically, he spoke as we went along. "Sometimes, the scent of a person can be a window into their soul. I can tell by the smell of these people what they're thinking. These are violent, evil men."

Kirsten walked along with her staff. It made a ringing noise every time it touched the trail. The trail went below a blue arch. It looked as if it were made of opaque glass blocks. Even the keystone was present. Nothing had a curve to it at all; everything was angles. At one point, a flood of small black dodecahedrons crossed the path. There was nothing for it but to walk among them. They parted around our feet without touching us.

"Are they alive?" I asked Wolf.

"They smell just like the other things in this place," he said, "I think that it is all alive to some extent." We continued on past the river of black things. The trail led us higher up one of the beige mountains. The mountain sloped steeply up on the right side, and steeply down on the left hand side. We turned a corner, and a green neon glow assaulted us.

There was a fence across the pathway. It consisted of a green neon post on the left hand cliff side, and horizontal bars springing from the post into the mountain. There appeared to be no way to climb around it in either direction.

Wolf sniffed at it cautiously, and jumped back. "It is like a cold flame that cuts," he said. "It will slice us in two if we try to pass through it."

I pondered the problem a little. "I guess we could go around, but that might take days, even if we didn't lose our way." We stood around and waited, as if by waiting a solution would come on its own.

Suddenly, Kirsten got angry. "They're not going to get away!" She yelled, and swung her staff at the fence. The fence flared and flickered, but the staff came away whole. She calmed down, and started to test the fence with vigor. She attacked it with the staff, both the post, and the bars. The post stopped the staff short, but the bars yielded and faded when the staff passed through them. However, they sprang back into being directly afterward.

Wolf spoke to Kirsten. "Hold a moment, child," he said. "Use the staff to block the horizontal bars coming from the post, all at once." She tried this, and was able to block almost all of the horizontal bars. But just as Wolf started forward, she gasped and let them spring back into place.

"There is a great force pushing me," she said. "I'm not sure if I can hold them." She looked at me, and I decided to try. I grabbed the staff and realized it was remarkably slippery, for all its rectangular shape. Wolf and Kirsten got ready to run through, as I neared the post. I put the staff in the way of the horizontal bars, and there was a fizzling sound, and I could feel the terrible cold near my hand. Wolf and Kirsten jumped through the gap safely, but I was still on the other side. The green fence was pushing me, as

I tried to rotate my body through the opening. As I made it through, the staff twisted, and the fence sprang back into place. I pulled the yellow staff through and gave it back to Kirsten. It was blackened in many places.

Kirsten took it and gasped in shock. "Listen!" She said. It was keening softly, as if in pain. "These shapes and objects must be alive!" Wolf nodded slowly.

I added a thought. "Alive or not, we're losing time. I think that we are falling behind them all this way." Kirsten agreed, and we set off at a faster pace. Soon we were descending the side of the mountain. On the uphill side of the mountain was a series of pentagonal brown logs. They all pointed down to the trail and lay on top of each other. They seemed in danger of becoming a landslide. We hurried through this area quickly. The mountain became foothills, and the foothills became a plain. The red trail spanned a small creek in the plain. We were all very thirsty. I took the first look at the creek, and noticed that the water was gritty. It didn't seem like there was grit in it, it seemed that the fluid itself was made up of tiny geometrical objects.

I looked at Wolf. "What do you think, Wolf? I'll drink it if you will."

He sniffed at it cautiously and then took a couple of laps. "It melts on the tongue," he said, "I'm not sure if it is water or not, but it will have to do. I don't think it is poisonous." Kirsten and I knelt down on the bank. We let it melt in our mouths purely for the sensation of letting it do so. We drank heavily regardless of the consequences, because you never know when you are going to get another drink of water. After this, we crossed the bridge and continued across the plain.

As we traveled the red path, we talked. Kirsten began. "Sometimes it seems that one thing leads to another, an endless chain of events that never stops."

"Until you die, I guess," I said. "Then who knows what happens."

Kirsten continued. "I like to think that when you die, your spirit becomes one with the rest of the energy of the world. In that way, you are still a part of everything that is happening."

"So when does the spirit begin?" I asked. "My first memory is when I was four years old. I was outside and a dragonfly landed on my hand. It was as big as my hand. That's all I can remember. Was that when I started having a spirit?"

She looked at me in disdain. "Are you saying that babies don't have a spirit? They have feelings and emotions just like you and me."

"I know that the forest has a spirit," I said rather meekly.

"Of course it does. Everything living has some kind of energy or spirit, if you'd like to call it that. Even babies in their mother's womb still have a spirit."

"I guess I know that. Do you really think that when you die that the spirit continues?"

"Well, I don't know for sure, but it seems like it must."

"I think that's a cop out. Your consciousness ends when your brain ceases to function. Just because you're feeling things at this moment doesn't mean that you will always feel things. Always and forever are abstract terms. They represent things, but not in life."

Kirsten thought a moment. "Isn't time forever?" She asked me.

"I don't think so." I said, "First of all, scientists think there was a time that the universe began. There was a massive, spontaneous burst of energy that created all the galaxies and planets. In my mind, we're just a part of the friction that is the gradual slowing down of the universe. As we move and collide, we use up the energy of the big bang, and eventually, nothing will move at all. Or at least, if things move, nothing happens to them any more. The suns die. At the point where nothing can affect anything anymore, time stops."

Kirsten looked interested. "That's pretty bleak. Do you have a time frame for that?"

"Oh about 10 to 80th power years from now."

"I see, so I don't need to worry about the sun collapsing any time soon," she teased. I responded quickly.

"Oh, on my world the sun will engulf the earth in only 5 billion years. We'll run out of oil and kill each other for energy sources long before then." We continued along the road in silence for awhile. There were some white cubes popping up in the air by the side of the trail. Kirsten's trusty staff still rang out against the glass-like surface of the trail. We were still on a plain, but ahead, we could see a large profusion of different colored columns. They speared high into the air, but they were still very far away. They jutted at strange angles, but seemed to have an order to them.

As we approached, the mass of angled columns looked more impressive. At the base of it, we could see small figures moving around. They were the men in orange jumpsuits and a familiar figure in black. It didn't seem that they had seen us yet. There were some purple pyramids off the trail, so we decided to hide ourselves between these. We tried to approach quickly, but soundlessly. Kirsten carried her staff instead of walking with it. Eventually we reached a point where the pyramids ran out, and there was nothing but plain between us and the people we had been following. We were fairly close, however, and we could see the black man gesturing with his crystal. The inmates seemed reduced in number, and looked recalcitrant. While we watched, the Borzhat priest lifted his crystal over one of the inmates, and passed it over his body. The inmate began to glow green and a look of ecstasy came over his face. He ran to the mound of angled columns and began to climb up to an opening not too far up the face of the columns. He entered the opening carefully. Kirsten whispered that we had to stop him, but I advised patience. The Borzhat priest was still, but the convicts waited restively. Soon, there was a drawn out cry of anguish from the mound of colored columns. Immediately, the convicts turned to the Borzhat priest and began arguing. He raised the crystal with his arms outstretched, and they cowered in fear.

At this point, we began to argue among ourselves quietly. Kirsten was all for attacking the priest and the convicts immediately, but there were at least seven that we could see, so I advised caution again. Wolf came up with the idea of entering the mass of columns ourselves to see what they were after. After the man had sounded like he had died horribly, Kirsten and I were not too keen on that idea. However, Wolf volunteered to go himself, even after we tried to dissuade him. He decided to circle around to another side to see if he could slip in unnoticed. We went with him to guard his entrance. He found an opening and climbed up to it and entered.

*   *   *   *   *

I smell the half-alive, half-dead smells of this place. Except for the bad men, everything smells exactly the same. It is a smell I have never encountered before. I don't see what is so different about the world here. Everything is the same. This is a small corridor. I walk down it slowly. There is moving air ahead. There is a place in the corridor that is moving without moving. It wishes to move. I can feel the walls tense as I pass. I think the half-life here knows that I respect life, and therefore lets me pass. I pass the wall quickly anyway. The floor slants down; it is hard to keep from sliding here. I brace my body against the wall, holding my legs straight. My leg still pains me a little. The one who helped me will always be my friend. There are spikes poking toward me at the end of the tunnel! I have to run toward them and jump to the side to miss them. I am clear. I am in a larger tunnel that smells of the bad men. It is the smell of evil and fear and blood. I turn away from the smell and head deeper into the mountain. Light makes its way through the mountain, but it is dim. I must rely on smell. This does not bother me. I walk along the larger corridor. The ceiling tapers to a point above me. I am walking in a triangle. The triangle continues for awhile. I smell moving air ahead of me and hesitate. I move slowly up to a break in the floor. It is a pit. It does not seem to be far to the other side. I circle and get a running start. I jump across! The air is warm from the pit. It seems to lift me up as I go. I am on the other side. The tunnel starts to slope up a little. I continue up the tunnel. Soon it is blocked. The tunnel is filled with small objects. I smell them. They are the same as everything else on this world. From a long way behind me, I hear a terrible scream. One of the bad men has died again. I start to dig at the mound of small objects. As soon as I move a few, the whole pile begins to shift. The little objects spill and roll down the tunnel towards me. Soon, I am swimming in the objects, trying to keep my footing. I cannot gain ground against the tide. I am being pushed back. I can hear the cascading of the objects over the lip of the pit. The sound is getting close. It is more of a not sound, as the objects fall into empty air. I struggle mightily against the avalanche. The objects are petering out. But my hind legs are pushed back over the edge of the pit. My belly is on the ground, and I cling to the ground as hard as I can. The avalanche has stopped, but I am partly over the pit. The floor of the corridor is too smooth. I can just barely reach the lip of the pit with one of my hind legs. Once this is accomplished, I can pull myself away from the pit. I try not to step on any of the small objects with my wounded leg. I make my way up the incline once again. The tunnel turns five sided at the top of the hill. There are stairs heading in many directions from here. All go up. I smell each carefully. All seem to reach open air but one. I decide to take the one stair that does not reach open air. I climb up the stairs. They turn and twist up. They get narrower and wider. They are not all even, but some are higher or longer. I must concentrate on climbing the stairs carefully. Then the stairs start going down. They are even and regular. After a while, they become wider. It is tempting to hurry down the stairs, but

I go even slower now. The stairs enter into a large room. It appears almost curved, but I think it just has many faces to it. I can barely detect a new smell here. It is wood. In the center of the room is a staff. It is standing straight up from a platform. There are almost circular stairs in the center of the room leading to the platform. I descend the final few stairs and start to mount the stairs to the platform. They are large, and I pull my body up the first one. I am frozen! A voice echoes in my head. "If your father is the head of the pack, but is old and not making decisions the way he used to do, do you challenge him for the leadership of the pack?" I am unsure what to do. My thoughts turn to the question. I would become leader of the pack, I am sure. I am able to move again. I climb up the next stair. As my body fully rests on the stair, I am frozen again. The same voice enters my head. "If you have a chance to destroy all the crystals on all the worlds, but you must let your friend die, would you destroy the crystals or save your friend?" This time I am not sure what to answer. I feel that whoever made these tests would want me to destroy the crystals, but I must answer honestly. "I would save my friend," I think to myself. My body is free to climb again. It takes effort to climb the next stair, and once again I am frozen. "If you are starving, and you happen upon a poor family with only one chicken, would you steal and eat that chicken?" This is truly a tough one. I have a great respect for people's right to live. However, I am starving. I think that I would eat the chicken and try to pay the family back later. I am not free to move! I try to think it forcefully to the voice. "I would eat the chicken and try to pay the family back later!" I am still not free to move. From the corner of my eye I see a skeleton above me, frozen on the next step. I must figure out the answer to the problem. I don't lie about eating the chicken, though. I think again to myself. "I would eat the chicken." This time, I am free to move. I consider going back down the steps. At least I have the information that the staff is safe. But, there are only a few more steps. I continue. Each step is an effort to climb. The next step freezes me again. The voice comes. "There is a cage. It is in bottomless mud. There is a group of people inside and a group of people on top of the cage. The weight of the people on top of the cage is pushing the cage into the mud. The men in the cage push their women to the top so they won't smother in the mud. The men on top of the cage gladly help the women out of the cage. Are you in the cage or on top of the cage?" Another easy one. "I am in the cage," I think to the voice. I am free to move. With effort, I climb another stair. The voice comes again. "Your bitch has gone over to a rival clan. She is now the rival clan leader's bitch. The only way to get her back is to start a clan war. Do you do so?" I think to myself. The bitch has dishonored me. But many will die in a clan war. I would not start a clan war over a female. I am free to move. One more step, and I will be able to reach the staff! I ascend the final platform. The voice stops me. "You have been running for days. You carry in your mouth the only medicine that can save your friend. Soon, you tire. You collapse to the ground, miles short of your goal. A wolf with no smell comes to you and listens to your story. He offers to carry the medicine to your friend. Do you give the medicine to him or try to drag yourself the final miles, knowing that you may be too late?" A wolf with no smell?

There is no such thing. I distrust this construct. I would drag myself the final miles. I am free to move again. I grab the staff between my teeth. It comes free with little resistance. A deep bell-like tone rings out. Suddenly, the column I am on lifts toward the ceiling. An opening is created there, and the column pushes me through it. Soon, I am in bright light at the top of the mountain. There are many pathways down, but it is all unshielded. I will try to hurry down the mountain before I am seen.

* * * * *

Wolf entered the mountain awhile ago. Kirsten and I waited unhappily among the purple pyramids, alternately watching Wolf's tunnel and the Borzhat priest. There had been several screams of inmates that had ventured into the crystal mountain, but so far, no howling from Wolf. I was visibly upset, and Kirsten took my hand to comfort me. I looked at her face, and especially her eyes. There was emotion there, as we both worried for Wolf. Her red hair was in disarray, but it prettily framed her face. She spoke to me quietly. "He saved my life, you know."

I nodded. "I've never had a friend like him. He seems so noble."

She drew closer to me and kissed me on the cheek. "He is noble," she said, "and you are great together."

I winced. "Then we should be together. I should be in there with him."

Kirsten held me around the waist. "He wanted to go alone. He thought he could succeed where others had failed." She looked up into my face, pressed so close to me. I looked down at her, and a moment of time began. It was like driving into a fog that comes from nowhere, and you don't know where to go. My head lowered to hers. At that moment, a bell-like sound reverberated from the mountain. We separated and peered between the pyramids. The Borzhat priest was screaming at the inmates. There were only four left. The priest gestured to the top of the mountain, and we saw what he did.

Wolf was coming down the mountain with a staff between his teeth! He was angling away from the priest and the inmates. The dissension between them stopped. They started to circle around the mountain to cut him off. Kirsten and I tried to circle around them, staying under the cover of the purple pyramids. Wolf ran down a turn, and disappeared from view around the back of the mountain. I stopped Kirsten.

"He's going to circle around the other way," I said. "Let's go back around this way." The priest and the inmates continued to run clockwise around the mountain, while we began to run widdershins. Soon the mountain blocked our view of the priest, and we came out into the open. We ran faster out from under the cover of the pyramids. After a while, we were around to the back side of the mountain. Wolf was down at our level! He saw us, and ran straight to us and dropped the staff at our feet. I crouched and gave him a huge hug. "I'm so glad you're all right," I said.

Kirsten had picked up the staff and was looking at it. It was carved all over with animals and trees, and the shadows of these carvings were burned on to the staff. She looked at me. "Here, you take it," she said. "I have my yellow one." I felt a little bit of panic at the responsibility she was handing me. I knew how she felt about the staff, and the act of her giving it to me was a grave one.

However, at that moment, the inmates and the priest came running around the mountain. They yelled and charged. I grabbed at the staff, and held it in front of me diagonally. Kirsten held her staff like a baseball bat. Wolf turned and leapt at the oncoming inmates. The priest raised his green crystal, and a fear washed over us. It was like being pushed underwater by a large wave. You struggle as the water roils around you, but you can't get to the surface, and you are running out of air. Wolf did not seem to feel the effects as he knocked one of the inmates into another. They both fell to the ground, and the first had his throat ripped out. The two other inmates passed Wolf and made their way to us. They took us on one on one. Both were thin and lean, but both looked stronger than we were. Kirsten swung her yellow staff at her combatant, but he jumped back out of the way. I tried to poke mine with the end, but he dodged as well, and grabbed the staff with his hands.

The priest shouted. "Bring me the staff! Untold wealth will be yours!" He started sketching in the air with his crystal. Wolf had turned around to help us, and the downed inmate had tackled him. It was a large, strong man, and Wolf was having trouble getting away. Kirsten's inmate had taken a blow to the side, but had wrapped his arm around the staff. He backhanded Kirsten, and she fell to the ground.

"No!" I shouted. I twisted my staff in a circle, breaking the other inmates grip on it. I stabbed him in the face with it and knocked his head back. He fell backwards and sat down. Kirsten's inmate had her yellow staff, and he swung it at me. I barely had time to block it, and he was swinging again and again. I reeled from the blows, falling backwards. Kirsten got up. She seemed dazed, but she walked quietly to our combat. I had tried getting in a few blows of my own, but the maniacal offense of the inmate was rendering me ineffective. Then Kirsten jumped on the legs of the inmate, and he stumbled. I quickly took advantage by hitting him as hard as I could in the hands. He cried out and dropped the yellow staff. Then I poked him in the stomach as hard as I could, and he fell to the ground.

We looked to Wolf quickly, but he had won his fight with the large inmate. Kirsten retrieved her staff. The inmate I had hit before got to his feet, but he looked dazed and unsure of himself. Wolf advanced on him and growled, and he backed away from us. The Borzhat priest completed sketching in the air, and another gateway appeared.

Kirsten yelled. "Wolf! Stop him!" Wolf leapt to the attack. The priest snarled, but didn't run. Instead he lifted the crystal. A green line traced through the air where the crystal had been. As Wolf sprang to attack, the priest jerked the line down like a whip. Wolf was tossed aside, with a big gash in his nose. We ran at the priest with our staffs, but before we could get there, Wolf was on the attack again. This time, he came in low, attacking the priest's legs. The priest scored Wolf's back with his glowing green whip, but Wolf bit into his leg. The priest's leather boots seemed to protect him from some of the damage, but he was thrown off balance. The inmate I had hit in the head had been running with us, and he grabbed Wolf from behind. Wolf let go of the priest, and Kirsten and I came up with our staffs. We circled the priest from two sides. The priest turned to face me, and he snapped his whip at me. I blocked it with the staff, but the glowing green line wrapped around the staff. He tried to jerk it away from me, but I held on for dear life. Then Kirsten hit him behind his head with the yellow staff. He fell to the ground and dropped his crystal. The glowing green line disappeared. Wolf had torn out the throat of his attacker, and he looked around for other opponents. The only inmate left was the one who I had poked in the stomach, and he looked unwilling to fight.

Kirsten went into a frenzy, and kept hitting the priest in the head with her staff. She wasn't very strong, but eventually it was clear that he was dead. Only then did Kirsten rest. I also rested, leaning on the staff of legend. It had been brought to battle once again. The inmate hesitantly came up to us. Wolf stood on point to guard him. He was lean and haggard, and looked untrustworthy.

"The priest drove us to it," he said. "All we wanted was our freedom, but he kept promising us riches and women if we would get the staff. Now that he's gone, I have no problem with you." Wolf growled, but I didn't want him to kill someone who was no longer attacking us.

I spoke to Wolf. "Leave him alone for now. Just guard him well."

Kirsten then spoke. "You have to destroy the crystal. It is a great evil, and we have the staff."

I looked skeptical. "Why do you think I can destroy it? Only that old man was able to do it."

"You have to try," she replied. "Use your will on it and wish that it was broken." I went to the crystal and raised the staff. I touched it lightly to the crystal and wished it were broken. It was unaffected. I tried focusing my thoughts on the crystal and concentrating as hard as I could. Still it remained unbroken. I brought the staff down upon the crystal with all my strength. It squirted away, but remained unbroken. I pounded it again and again to no avail. I rested the staff on the crystal and let my thoughts wander for a moment. I thought of The Dugouts, and the first time that I had seen them. I thought of being transported to the endless forest. I remembered the promise I had made to the forest spirit to respect the forest. Then there was a cracking sound at my feet. A small crack had appeared in the green crystal. The inmate behind us cried out.

"You're doing it!" Kirsten cried. I concentrated harder, specifically thinking of the faith I had that trees had a harmony that is special. I promised to do everything I could to keep that harmony intact. The crystal shattered with a sound like glass breaking. The inmate cried out again and slumped to the ground. The pieces of the crystal liquefied and evaporated into steam. Kirsten jumped up and hugged me.

"You did it! You're like the hero of legend! We have to tell someone." This didn't excite me all that much, as the life of a hero seemed somewhat fraught with responsibility. I looked to Wolf who was sniffing at the collapsed inmate.

The inmate looked as if he couldn't move. Sure enough, he was a pile of boneless flesh. A breathy moan emerged from the mass. Kirsten was disgusted. "He's still alive? How can that be?" Without much discussion, it seemed obvious that the only thing to do was to kill him. Wolf grabbed him by the throat and bit through it. The inmate died quickly. I was wondering what to do next, when we all sort of turned to the gate that the priest had made. It was similar to the other one we had seen, but this one showed us a different world. This gate opened on to a flat featureless plain. Occasional circular pools of water were the only things to unbalance the landscape. The sky above was a bright blue with scattered clouds.

I was the first to speak about the other world. "I think we should continue our journey and explore this world. We can always retrace our steps if we have to. However, I'm about to drop from exhaustion. I have to get some sleep." Kirsten and Wolf agreed, and we settled down near but not too near the gate to the other world.

Chapter 7

"Greatest fools are oft most satisfied."
Nicholas Boileau-Despreaux, Satire 4

I was the last to arise after our sleep, and I was cold from the missing body heat of the others. Wolf was nosing around the body of the priest.

"There is some food in his pockets," he said. "It is travel food, dried and uninteresting. I do not want any, but you and Kirsten may want it." Kirsten and I found it and gratefully took the edge off of our hunger. We saved some of it, because the other world seemed featureless. After a moment's hesitation, we decided to travel to the other world. Wolf went first to scout the way. He disappeared from view for a moment as he circled the gate, but then inclined his head toward us. He seemed to be moving slowly. Kirsten went next, still hanging on to her yellow staff, and I went last with the staff of legend. My first impression of the place was the effort it took to move. Every motion was an effort. To walk was like being stuck in slow motion.

All around us was nothing but plain in every direction. Small circular pools dotted the plain, and they were remarkable in their geometry. Each was as perfect a circle as you would care to draw. We gathered slowly around the nearest. It reflected our inquisitive faces back at us. Wolf bowed his head and lapped at the water, and soon Kirsten and I were cupping handfuls of it to our faces as well. It seemed disproportionately deep, but it reflected the sky, so we could not see anything underneath the surface. After our thirst was quenched, we looked around at the plain again. There seemed to be no difference to our choices, so we just set off in the direction the gate faced.

We traveled on for miles. It was extremely slow going, and we tired quickly. There was no sun in the sky to guide our travels, but the plain was straight, and we could keep to a fairly straight line. Wolf assured us that he would be able to track our way back to the gate barring a deluge. That seemed unlikely as the clouds were wispy and non-threatening. Kirsten began to make noise about going back to the world where everyone slept rather than continuing this difficult and apparently useless journey. I argued that there must be someone here if the priest wanted to make a gate to this place. Kirsten argued that I knew nothing of gates and had no idea what I was talking about. Wolf stayed silent during these exchanges, and our forward impetus continued.

After another long while, it seemed that the circular pools of water were becoming more numerous. Some were larger, and some clustered closer together. We drank again, but saved our food, even though it was long past time for eating. Then Wolf sniffed in the air and declared that there was something ahead. We deviated from our straight line to explore it. Wolf led the way. We found a cylindrical tube of water leading from one of the pools away to an area where no pools were near. It was not very large, maybe six inches in diameter, but it lay in a straight line for a hundred yards. The tube was murky, and we could smell what Wolf smelled. The tube ended in a plume of waste on the plain. It just emptied out on to the ground. The area smelled terrible, and we could imagine that Wolf was suffering even more with his heightened sense of smell. Since it was the only landmark we had come across, we examined it carefully, but we couldn't imagine that anyone would live near here. We decided to travel back to where the pools were becoming more frequent.

Wolf was glad enough to get away from the waste. We traveled back close to our original bearing. Soon, the pools were as frequent as the plain we walked on. We could hear splashing ahead of us. This excited us, and we tried to increase our pace against the molasses of this world's physics. Ahead of us, we could see a strange sight. There was a fountain of balls of water leaping out of one of the larger pools. The globes leapt from the pool quickly, and slowed as they rose into the air. Then they returned to the pool with a splash. They were only about a foot in diameter, and they made small shrieking sounds as they rose and fell in the air. Occasionally one of the water globes would hover in the air for a moment, and move sideways before plunging back into the pool.

We watched in fascination for awhile, wondering what the purpose of this fountain of globes could be. Then one of the globes moved nearer to us and shrieked in a higher tone. It quickly disappeared back in to the pool. A few more globes popped out of the water, but soon they disappeared back into the pool. In a moment, a larger globe slowly surfaced in the water, not leaving the pool but staying near the bank where we stood. Then it submerged, and the pool was empty again. Kirsten was the first to speak.

"I think those globes of water saw us, and are intelligent," she said. "They must live in the pools of water." A whole group of large half globes surfaced in the pool. I heard a voice in my mind.

"We have paid our tribute of water," it said. "Why do you come to bother our children?" I looked at Wolf, and he nodded to me. He had heard the voice as well.

I took it upon myself to speak. "We did not come to bother your children," I said. "We are traveling through this land looking for a way home to our kind."

Another voice spoke in our heads. "You under-dwellers always desire our water. You threaten us with dissolution if you do not get what you want. We have given our quota of water for the month, and we wish you to leave us alone."

Kirsten replied for us this time. "We are not the same as the ones who take your water. We are individuals ourselves. Besides, we are not under-dwellers."

The original globe spoke again. "Do you not survive under the water? You solid creatures have always lorded over the watery kind."

I was unsure what to say to convince him. "We mean you no harm. If you could guide us to our own world, we would gladly leave you in peace."

The globes responded as one. "We will confer." They sunk down into the pond.

Kirsten looked at the pond and then came up with an idea. "Do you think the Borzhat have been extracting tribute from these creatures? After all, the priest did open a gate here."

I seized on the idea. "Yes, it seems quite possible. They would be the kind to subjugate a race for their assets." Fresh water is surely a valuable commodity to some people.

The water globes resurfaced. "We will guide you to our elder wizard. He will know what to do."

"How will you guide us?" Kirsten asked. "We cannot follow you under water."

The globe laughed a little. "We will plunge into the pools ahead of you and show ourselves to you," he said. They disappeared beneath the pool again, and after a little while, a globe half surfaced in a pool far ahead of us. We trudged our way through the thick air, or whatever it was, and made it to the pool. The globe sank, and another appeared almost instantly, far ahead of us to the right. We circled the ponds on our way to the other pool. When we got there, it disappeared and another surfaced ahead of us. We followed the globes a half a dozen times or more, and soon we were at a small pool off by itself. The globe spoke to us this time. "Wait here for a moment," it said. "The elder wizard Knossis will be with you shortly."

After a minute, a large globe surfaced with a smaller globe behind him. "I am Knossis!" It said in our minds. "This is my apprentice, Krovis. What do you want of our humble people?"

We had said that we wanted to find a way home, so I stuck to that idea. "We have been attacked by the Borzhat. For the most part, we were victorious, but now it is time to be getting home. We may have a valuable tool that could be used to defeat them."

The large globe seemed to think a moment. "In that case, come up to the dwelling. I can make it so the water does not choke you here." The two globes disappeared below the water. I decided to stick my head under the water to see where they were going. I kept my eyes open underwater and looked into their 'dwelling.' It was as if a sphere of water under the ground just touched the surface at the junction of the pond. There were tubes of colored water flowing in and out of the walls of the place. The two globes could still be seen, hovering in the water. I took a small sip of water, but I swallowed it instead of breathing it in. I tried doing so again, and this time it seemed I could breathe the water in the room. I lifted my head out. " I t seems okay, guys. Let's dive in and talk to… uh, Knossis." This time, I led the way. I took most of my clothes off, and dove into the pool. I kept the staff with me as it seemed to be too valuable to leave outside the dwelling. Strangely, once I was in the dwelling I was free to move more easily. The water was wet, but it moved about me like air. I was floating in space, but I could move by making swimming motions. I took a tentative breath, and I could ingest the water. Kirsten came splashing in next, and then Wolf. All of us were floating in mid-water, thankful that we were able to move freely for the first time in awhile. There was a large opening in one side of the dwelling. It led off back in the direction we had come.

Knossis rippled and spoke in our minds. "How do we know this is not a trick of the enemy to test our obeisance? Never have the under-worlders been good to us. Always you threaten to kill us if we do not give you water." We floated around slowly, having to swim in the thin water constantly to keep our orientation.

I showed him the staff. "This staff has been used in the past to destroy the crystals of our enemy. Their eyes leak fire, and they are cruel. It is important that we get this staff into the right hands."

Knossis said nothing for a time, and then the smaller globe Krovis came forward. "It is I who am the real wizard here. Knossis is my apprentice. Few even on this world know that fact, for we have held the secret a long time. Knossis, you must not broadcast the news of the staff. There are many on this world that would be for turning these travelers over to the Borzhat." He spoke again to us. "We will keep your secret and help you travel to another world friendlier to your kind." The two globes began floating to different areas on the walls. They touched the colored tubes and absorbed some of the color into their bodies. There were reds, yellows, greens, and blues. These colors stayed distinct in their bodies and flowed around each other. Soon the globes were swirling rainbows. Krovis spoke again. "You must get your things. It is a long journey, and you must stay close to us while we travel. Otherwise, you will not be able to breathe the water up here." Kirsten and I exited back up to the thick air, and dressed in our dry clothes. Then we plunged back into the pool. We were on our way.

The multi-colored globes led us down a rock passageway. Krovis made a yellow glowing light that trailed out behind him as he moved through the tunnel. Knossis brought up the rear. There were many branchings in the tunnel, but Krovis seemed to know where to go. Sometimes the rock was covered with soft looking fungus or coral. The yellow light threw shadows on the strange shapes. Krovis spoke in our minds.

"I am taking seldom used tunnels to avoid meeting others, but if we swim into someone, you must not speak." We agreed to be silent if the occasion arose. Occasionally, we swam into a chamber. The process for this was always the same. Krovis would swim up to the opening and request entrance. When there was no response, we would swim into the large round room. There were never any colored tubes of water as in the wizard's domain. Sometimes there were concave objects that looked like they might serve as beds or chairs for these watery globes. Often there was vegetation on the walls, whether decorative or functional I did not know. We had traveled through a half dozen of these chambers when Kirsten spoke. "I'm getting tired. I'm not used to swimming all this distance." I was tired too and said so.

Krovis spoke in our minds again. "All right, we'll find a chamber out of the way and rest for awhile." He made a turn, and requested entrance at a chamber down the tunnel. There was no reply, and we entered a small dwelling. "It will be difficult for you to sleep in the water," Krovis said. "Please let me give you something to help you sleep." Wolf growled slightly, but he looked tired too.

I shrugged my shoulders. "If that's what you think is best. We're in your hands." Krovis moved toward us, and a blue stream issued from his globe body. It was a short distance to my face. The stream wound its way to me, and I breathed it in. I felt nothing at first, but then a warm tingly feeling came over me. I sank to the bottom of the dwelling and remembered nothing more.

*   *   *   *   *

I was slow to wake up, groggy. Krovis urged us to move more quickly this day.

"The news of your coming has been broadcast on the currents," he said. "Most are uninterested, but there are some that will remember and think to tell the Borzhat. I hope they do not visit our world soon." That got us moving quickly enough, and we swam to follow Krovis down the passageway. We swam on for a long time, going through dwellings occasionally. Krovis requested entrance at one dwelling, and was answered. A quick white stream of color emerged from his body and surrounded Wolf, Kirsten, and me. It surrounded us, and started coalescing into globes.

The voice from the dwelling spoke again. "Please enter. Why do you wait?" Krovis entered, and we followed. There was a medium sized globe inside. Many different colored plants grew from the walls. "Five of you are a lot to feed, but you are welcome." Krovis and Knossis both sent words of agreement. We remembered our promise to be silent and said nothing. The stranger spoke again. "Why are these globes silent, and so strangely white? Why are you so colorful?"

Knossis replied. "We are the shepherds for these old ones. The colors are our badges of office. We take them to their final destination. They are senile and cannot speak. We will let their flows become one with the current."

The stranger accepted this. "Will they take nourishment? I am glad to share my food with them."

Knossis replied again. "Yes, I believe they will do so. We have traveled far already." The stranger introduced himself as Kivless. He pulled some orange plants off of the wall and set them free in the middle of the room. Krovis and Knossis absorbed some of these plants, and pushed others in our direction. As they touched outside of our spheres, they were absorbed as well. I grabbed one and started chewing. It was a mushy tasteless thing, but I was very hungry. I ate all that came into my sphere. Then I ate some of the travel food I still had left.

Kivless was quite animated. "I've never seen anyone so old that they were white," he said. "They cannot speak? Their state is so sad, but it will be a blessing once they join the current."

Knossis made agreeable thoughts and then asked a question. "Are we close to the great chasm? This is where we plan to release the old ones."

Kivless answered. "Yes, this is the last outpost before the chasm. The gate is right beyond my dwelling."

Knossis let his intentions be known. "We must go then to the chasm. Thank you for a wonderful meal, but we must be off." Krovis led the way out, and we followed silently. Knossis thanked the host again and again as Kivless tried to insist that we stay. We got away though, and made our way down the tunnel. Soon we came to a metal gate that covered the entire passageway. The openings in it were too small to even get a hand through. Krovis sent a stream of purple liquid at the gate, and it creaked on its vertical hinges. It pivoted and made an opening on both sides large enough for us to get through. Krovis could get through without any trouble, but Knossis had to squeeze to a thinner shape to get through.

Knossis grumbled. "Squeezing through the gate and going to the chasm for a few underdwellers. It's not decent, I say."

Krovis hushed him. "Actually, we are going to have to cross the chasm. To my knowledge, it hasn't been done since the separation of the Kinter clan." I had no idea who the Kinter clan was, but after seeing the gate and hearing

101

the attitude of Knossis, I was a little worried. Krovis closed the gate with another wash of purple. We continued to make our way down the passageway, following Krovis's yellow stream of light. The passageway grew rougher, and it widened out. Eventually, it became a ledge opening onto a bottomless gap. Our white globes were dispersing and were sucked into the chasm.

Krovis spoke into our minds quietly. "There are creatures here, the Tentalwhin and the Endlemor. I will use a very little light, so that you can follow me, but you must be quiet. They are very dangerous, and can drive us to dissolution. They are some of the only creatures besides your kind who kill for the joy of killing."

Krovis started across the chasm, spilling a little light from his body. Only enough for us to follow. It dripped slowly into the chasm and went out. It felt like the dark is rising. We swam carefully and quietly after him, and Knossis brought up the rear. The isolation was oppressive. After the close tunnels we had passed through, the open ended nothing put us on edge. I felt as if the whole of the ocean was watching us, and I almost asked Krovis to put out the light.

We swam on and on. We entered a forest of floating pink seaweed. We swam in between the strands, glad of the cover. Then Kirsten let out a small cry. Her leg had become entangled in a couple of the long pieces. She thrashed around a little trying to get loose, and the seaweed pulled and twisted. There was a hissing sound from below us. A large group of eels swam vertically right through our party.

"Endlemor!" Knossis cried, and moved toward

Kirsten. Krovis made a bright circular yellow light, and the eels scattered. Kirsten was grabbing at her leg trying to get free of the seaweed. Suddenly, the eels were among us again. They had flat dead eyes, and an underbite, with sharp teeth protruding. I poked my staff toward one, and it grabbed on to the end and didn't let go. The eels dived and swooped around us. One took a bite out of Wolf's flank, and he howled. Krovis and Knossis were shooting red balls of goo at the eels. If a ball hit the head of one, it was covered, and swam away. The eel that was holding my staff wiggled fiercely, and started biting its way up the staff. I noticed that Wolf was snapping at the eels that passed him by, sometimes tearing one in two. I punched at my eel, and it let go of the staff and started in on me. It bit me on the thigh, on the stomach, and then I grabbed it around the head. It slipped free and circled around the battle again, but I lost it, because there were many more.

Krovis and Knossis continued to shoot the red balls, and some eels were affected, but not enough. I swam for Kirsten to free her. One of the eels took a bite out of my arm and swam away again. I was leaving a small trail of blood in the water. I got to Kirsten, and pulled at the seaweed around her ankle. I had to tear it, but it came apart soon. She was crying and waving her arms as the eels attacked her especially. For some reason, I glanced up, and I saw a ghostly outline of a globe coming down toward us. Suddenly, a searing white light burst from the globe, and I had to turn away. The eels hissed in pain, and swam down away from the light. The light expanded and floated down between us, too bright to look at. As it sunk below us, it started to dim, but the eels were long gone.

Krovis spoke. "We must go immediately. We have bloodied the water here, and will attract many dangerous creatures." He released some of the sticky red balls on our wounds, and we swam away through the seaweed.

"What was that light?" I asked Krovis.

"There are many strange things in the chasm," he replied. "Now be quiet, we do not want to attract any more Endlemor." We swam on in silence, eventually coming to open water again. I noticed that the red and yellow colors were mostly gone from the two globes, and it gave me reason for concern. We swam for hours. It was at least as far as we had come through the tunnels before we reached the other side of the chasm. We came right up to a ledge like the one we had left. We swam into a rough tunnel that continued straight out for awhile.

"The gates are near now," said Krovis. "We must find the one that is best for you." The tunnel sloped up gradually. Soon branchings spurred off of the main tunnel. "Just ahead," said Krovis. Suddenly, he halted. There was a blue glow in front of him. A voice spoke in the water.

"Ahh, I see you escort humans to the gates. Dangerous work, especially now that you have run into me." It was a Borzhat priest. He had a blue globe around his head and a blue crystal in his hand.

Krovis replied. "Be careful, evil one, you are one and we are five." The priest raised his crystal and snarled. Immediately, Krovis and Knossis fired red globes at him. The globes stuck to the blue light surrounding the priest's head, but did nothing more than impede his vision a little. The priest slammed his crystal into the rock floor of the passageway. A blue light flashed, and a loud crack was heard. The rock below the priest's feet split, and water started rushing into the gap. The priest settled to the floor with his feet on both sides of the break in the rock. The water around us started pulling us toward him. Air began to appear above our heads in the ceiling of the tunnel. Both Krovis and Knossis fired red globes at the crack, but it was too large. The red globes were merely sucked into the gap.

Krovis yelled in our minds. "That gap will destroy our kind, and we cannot survive in air. We must flee! I'm sorry I cannot do more to protect you." He threw out a large yellow globe of light. Then they swam back down the tunnel as the turbulent water lowered. Wolf used the water's momentum to leap at the priest. He burst out of the water as it was lowering and tried to bite the priest's throat. His jaws were somehow blocked by the blue globe around the priest's head. The priest slashed at Wolf with the crystal, but Wolf leapt away. I used my staff to help steady myself in the swirling water, and the priest looked at me.

"Yes, I see why the treasonous globes were bringing you here now. What is it that you fear?" The blue smoke coming from where his eyes should be seemed to brighten, and I felt searching fingers at the corners of my mind. The weight of the stone above my head threatened to overwhelm me. The fear of the power of an unknown enemy entered my mind. Suddenly, dragged from my mind, another horrible thought entered my head. I feared having no one else to turn to. I feared knowing no one around me, and living in isolation. Kirsten and Wolf disappeared. Only the priest and I remained. He smiled but did not move. His crystal glowed more brightly as a line began to drip from it. Loneliness began to overwhelm me. Somehow I knew if I gave the staff to the priest that he would befriend me and take care of me. He was the only one in the world that still cared about me. My hands began to release the staff, but I was moving in slow motion. At that moment, the thought of Wolf entered my head. I had helped him, and ever since that moment, he had been my steadfast companion. I remembered his brave act of entering the geometric mountain alone. I remembered him circling below me as I was lifted into the sky by a braid of hair. I tightened my grip on the staff, and the smile disappeared from the priest's face. Suddenly a whip of blue light had appeared in his hands, and Wolf was jumping at him again.

The whip took Wolf in the side of the head, and he was knocked away. Kirsten ran up, but had to stay out of the whip's range. The water now had reached the level of the crack in the rock, and was not draining any more. I was down the tunnel a small ways, thigh deep in water. I splashed out of the water, climbing toward the priest, but he flicked the whip in my direction. Wolf tried to get to his feet, and the Borzhat priest flailed away at him with the whip. He was laying open large cuts, but Wolf only howled, never yelped. I rushed the priest again, this time holding my staff out in front of me. The priest snaked the whip out at my legs, but I jumped over it and hit him with the right end of the staff. He took a blow to the shoulder, but raised the whip back for another strike. Kirsten flew in and grabbed his arm as it was raised, and he could not effectively swing it at me. I hit him again and again in the stomach with the staff, and he doubled over. I hit him in the back, and the globe around his head disappeared. I hit him in the head, and he dropped the crystal. The fire in his eyes went out.

Kirsten leaned on me, breathing hard. I turned to look at Wolf, and he was struggling to his feet. He was bleeding badly from cuts along his flank. I walked over to the crystal and kicked it a little way away from the unmoving priest. Then I thought of the tree spirit and my promise to respect the forest. I hit the crystal with the staff and it broke into pieces and dissolved. The priest's body collapsed with a sigh. Then the smoke from the dissolved pieces of the crystal began to coalesce. The form of a hooded face took shape from the smoke. The only visible features of the face were two smoky eyes, recessed deep in the hood.

A voice spoke in our minds. "Destroying pieces of the Primus crystal will be punished by torture and death. I see you have the staff of the enemy. It will be of no avail. We are creating a disease which will spread to every world until the universe is ours." A wave of despair passed over us, but it dissipated with the smoky visage.

"Who do you suppose that was?" Kirsten asked.

I took a stab at it. "It must have been one of the leaders of the Borzhat, perhaps their archpriest."

Wolf spoke then for the first time in a long while. "There are three archpriests of the Borzhat," he said. "Each has a different colored crystal. I had never believed the legend until we started meeting them." The yellow globe that Krovis had left was lighting our surroundings, but it grew dark quickly outside of the immediate area. I pushed my staff into the globe, and some of the yellow light stuck on the staff. We took all of the priest's food again and started to explore.

"I wonder which gate we were supposed to use," Kirsten commented. We explored side tunnels and found three watery looking vertical circles. For any other exploration we would have had to dive back underwater, and we were pretty sure that we would not be able to breathe without Krovis' help. We decided to plunge through the nearest gate and see what awaited us.

❖ Chapter 8

"Innumerable as the stars of night, or stars of morning, dewdrops which the sun impearls on every leaf and every flower."
John Milton, Paradise Lost

We could not see what lay on the other side of the gate. All we could see was the watery surface of a circle. Wolf was willing to leap through into the unknown and then check back with us to tell us what was on the other side. He gathered himself, and splashed through the gate. Kirsten and I waited for his return, but all was silent.

Kirsten worried. "He must be hurt. The world on the other side of the gate may be uninhabitable."

I responded. "Well, I'm not leaving him alone. I'm going to go through as well, no matter what happens."

She agreed. "Yes, of course, I guess that's the only thing to do." She looked at me with an intense gaze. "Do you think this is it?"

I shook my head. "No, we'll be alright. I promise." Instinctively, we held hands, and then jumped through together. Into darkness. It was pitch black with open spaces all around us. The ground was smooth and black, like obsidian. It was quite cold on this world.

Wolf was there, and he spoke. "There is no way back. The gate is closed on this side."

Kirsten sighed hopelessly. "I hope this is the right way then. Somehow, prospects don't seem good." I had to agree with her. The light from my staff threw dim reflections on the strange black waves of glass around us. There was a path leading away from the gate uphill. As it was the only choice, we decided to follow it. The path was smooth, but not slippery, although I imagined if it rained it might be a different story. The path almost seemed like it might be a track for storm water, coming down the mountain. Most of the time, the sides of the trail were thigh high on us. We climbed up the trail, in single file. Wolf led the way, Kirsten followed, and I brought up the rear. As we reached higher elevations, snow started to flurry. The staff shone its small circle of light, and the flakes of snow falling into that circle were black. This anti-snow didn't accumulate yet, but kept stinging us with small cold kisses. Wolf laid his ears back at the weather, but he was the one most protected from it.

After a while, we came to a plateau. It was high in the mountains, but strangely silent. No wind blew over the top of the mountain. It was almost perfectly circular. We were tired from the long day in the watery world, and our shorter stretch here. It seemed a good place to huddle together and sleep for awhile. The smooth glassy surface was hard and flat, but there were no imperfections in the dark material to jut into our backs. We curled up together with Kirsten in the middle to protect her most from the cold. Slowly we drifted off to sleep. As I slept, I dreamed.

The sky cleared of its looming clouds. The stars began to show themselves. The brightest appeared first, then the dimmer ones. The Milky Way spread across the night sky, a faint road of dim stars. The normal northern constellations appeared. The Big Dipper, Orion, Cassiopeia. Then the stars appeared to move. They started crawling across the sky, not in circles, but in lines in every direction. The Milky Way became fatter and brighter, as it appeared to get closer. Wispy clouds of dust or gas blew past us. The sky became brighter as more and more stars appeared. Eventually, there was a terrible blackness in the sky. A circular hole from which no light escaped. It grew larger and larger, until there were no stars visible in the sky. A voice was heard.

"We don't have time for this. Their battle threatens to intrude upon our own."

Another voice chimed in, almost identical to the first. "A world on the edge," it said. "These may be the ones to save it."

Either the first voice or some other voice also added its opinion. "They must take care of business and not let the evil escape into the universe."

Voices continued. "The enemy is marching together in a hive mind. I fear it will overwhelm the ones who resist."

"The time for the ultimate answer is not yet ripe. They still have a chance to defeat the enemy on their world."

"The time for the ultimate answer grows near. A truly powerful hive mind on their world will strengthen the darkness in our battle."

"The balance tips in the favor of evil. Power for power's sake is on the rise. We wish we could do something to help them physically."

"They lie on the obsidian plateau. We can send them anywhere."

"To the world where the battle will be joined then."

The voices seemed to speak to us for the first time. "If your battle spills out of your world, we will invoke the ultimate answer. Good luck, and do not try to reach us again." Stars appeared once again at the edges of the sky. They swarmed toward the center of the circle of darkness and became bright. The Milky Way appeared again, and dominated the sky. It faded away slowly to a faint ribbon, and the stars became dimmer and dimmer until they disappeared entirely. A soft red glow appeared above us, and I realized I was awake.

At first I thought the red glow might be the early light of dawn, but above me I saw, not a sky, but a high roof supported by trusses. Kirsten and Wolf were awake as well, and Kirsten spoke. "Those voices, they sent us somewhere."

I was not too surprised that the others had shared my dream. "Yes, they seem to think that our battle will be joined here. I wonder where we are." We looked around. We appeared to be in an old warehouse, but there was a stage built at one end. This is where the red light was coming from, there were lights focused on the stage. There were instruments typical of a rock band set up. Just as we were wondering if they might be familiar, Danno, the bass player for The Dugouts came through a doorway from the side of the stage.

"I thought I heard voices," he said. "Is the front door open or something? Oh, it's you guys. There's the big wolf. How did it go after the prison break?"

I looked at Kirsten and she laughed. "It's been quite an adventure," she said. "Look, we have the staff of legend. We've already broken crystals with it." Danno looked impressed.

"Broken crystals, hey? That brings a new hope to us. I'd never have believed it would happen in my

113

lifetime. There's a new problem here though. Something is happening in the wilderness of Africa that is concerning everyone. No one knows what's really happening out there, but we've got to go to find out. We're having a concert tonight to spread the word." I was holding out the staff of legend for him to inspect, and he looked at it carefully.

"Well, it's certainly beautiful enough to be the staff of legend. Look at all these carvings. Here's a wolf. It looks just like you, old boy. The recessed areas are burned black, too." He began to hand the staff back to me. I held up my hands.

"Why don't you keep it?" I said. "You are the ones who have been battling the Borzhat all this time."

Danno shook his head. "No, you're the one who destroyed the crystals. It is not a sure thing that any of us could do it." He handed the staff to me. I took it reluctantly. It seemed that I would have to bear the responsibility for a while longer. We asked Danno where we were, and he explained that we were in a warehouse in downtown Manhattan. It happened to be close to the East Village. We decided to spend some of the day touring the village while we waited for the Dugouts to play. We kept a careful eye on where the warehouse was so we could find it again. The door was painted red.

First we went north until we reached the park. It was not large, and we decided not to actually enter the park. Instead, we then walked west along St. Mark's Place. There were vintage clothing stores and music stores. There were used book shops and coffee houses. We went into a coffee house and had some pastries. Even Wolf deigned to eat some of the confections. He must have been very hungry.

We had plenty of time to kill, so we sat on the couches. On the table next to us was some kind of oil fountain. It had light in the center of it, and wires coming down from the top in straight lines. Oil spilled out of the top and ran down in beads down the wires. The beads of oil picked up the light and sparkled as they fell. Unlike a fountain, it was completely silent. Kirsten picked up a newspaper that was on the table next to her.

"Look, it's in the news! Portions of Africa have been completely cut off from communication. Not the cities, but some of the people of the villages in the Rift Valley have lost all contact with the outside world. Strange tales of mass murders have been coming from these villages."

I looked sharply at Kirsten. "Is that the Post or the Times?" I said. She handed the paper to me. I looked at the article as well. It was strangely uninformative. We killed some more time in the coffeehouse and then made our way out into the streets again. We had the feeling in the streets that we had to find a place to hang out in, and when we found a place to hang out, there was the feeling that we had to move along. Eventually we entered a music store that looked appealing. There was very little space between the racks of music. Wolf's tail was constantly knocking the CD's around. We looked for a CD by The Dugouts, but were disappointed when we couldn't find one. We weren't sure whether to ask the man behind the counter about them either. We didn't see any flyers about the show in the store window, but then we hadn't seen any flyers about the band in our whole time walking around the East Village. We decided to leave without buying anything, as there was sure to be merchandise for sale at the show tonight.

After we left the music shop, we were undecided about where to go. We still had about six hours to kill. Kirsten piped up. "I've never been to this world. I want to see a museum."

I had kind of wanted to go to Washington Square Park to play chess, but I was amenable. "Okay, let's take the subway up to the Metropolitan Museum of Art." We asked around, and the nearest subway was at Park Ave. and St. Mark's Place. Wolf elicited no comment on the subway, or anywhere else for that matter. Either the people of New York had seen it all, or perhaps he just somehow escaped notice. He didn't have to pay for a spot on the subway, or at the museum. The museum seemed like it had a hundred steps going up to the front entrance, spreading in all directions. We went into the large atrium and grabbed a map from the information booth. I advised going to the Egyptian wing first. The numerous artifacts from the days of the pharaohs were splendid and interesting. I especially liked the tiny colorful scarabs that were on display. We finished up that wing by entering the large windowed room that had the vault that was actually moved from Egypt to the museum. It was a mammoth structure you could enter, and it had hieroglyphs. Kirsten was suitably impressed.

We toured the rest of the museum, looking at porcelain from ancient China, and European portraits. One of the more restful moments came when we found an out of the way spot. It was a bench in a Japanese wing in front of a fountain. We enjoyed sitting there for awhile. There was also American Indian history, and statues. It was all too much to take in over the span of a few hours. As much walking as we had done on other worlds, we were starting to get tired. So we decided to take our leave of the museum and find some dinner.

I assumed my credit card would still work. Since I was embroiled in a fight that I seemed unlikely to survive, I decided to treat the others to a nice dinner and save our scant supply of cash. Normally I loathe piling up credit debt. It's a way of burying yourself deep financially that doesn't seem to take any of your money. But those interest rates pile up your debt, and if you ever miss a payment, watch out! We walked around the east side of Manhattan looking for a place to eat. We found a nice restaurant on the second floor of a building. It was a Japanese steakhouse where they cook the food in front of you. Wolf, Kirsten, and I had to share our table with five others. If they minded sharing the table with a wolf, they didn't say anything. First, the waitress took our order. I ordered steak and fish for myself, and steak with extra steak for Wolf. Kirsten ordered the Emperor dinner, which was Filet Mignon, shrimp, and lobster. I winced a little bit, because my credit card already had a large balance on it. Now that we were at the restaurant, and on my own world, I was considering just flying back to ------ to continue my job. I wondered what the date was, and whether I had missed my first day of work. If time had passed at all concurrently, I had probably missed my first week, and was fired. I still had my boss's card in my wallet, and I resolved to call him. I decided not to let the problems I had spoil my dinner.

First course was a clear chicken broth that was delicious. Wolf spilled his all over the table while lapping it up, but licked it off the table. A salad was next, which was unremarkable except for the dressing. The house dressing was a ginger, and it was also good. Then the main course came. A chef with a trolley came out to our table. He cooked cabbage, sweet carrots, and fried rice, along with our main orders. It was quite a show. He tossed his knife and spatula around, and spun the salt and pepper shakers while he seasoned the food. It was all excellent. I paid the waitress and left a good tip. I knew she had to split her tip 50/50 with the chef. By then, we figured it was time to get back to the warehouse and get ready to see The Dugouts play.

We took the subway back downtown, and walked down St. Mark's Place again. Now that it was night, the place had a brighter, more exciting feel to it. There were T-shirt and hat stands lit up with bright lights. Most of the stores were still open to cater to the later evening crowd. As we hit the park, we turned south to find the warehouse again. Unfortunately, when we got there, we saw a depressing sight. There was a line going all the way around the block to get in. It wasn't just single file either, it was five people wide. We passed some freaky looking people on our way to the back of the line. After turning two corners around the block, we found the end of the line. We stood in it, and the inevitable questions started. Kirsten started the barrage. "Have they started letting people in yet? I haven't seen any movement in the line."

A burly looking, grey haired biker with a big moustache turned around. "I heard that the place is already full and it's one in, one out."

"What?" Kirsten exclaimed. "They'll never get this many people into that place if it's already full. Have they started playing yet?"

The biker responded. "Well, I don't hear anything, and it's pretty early. I don't think they've started."

Kirsten frowned and slumped a little. "This is horrible. We'll never get in." People were already beginning to line up behind us. I wondered how many of them knew The Dugouts and how many of them were just lining up to be in line. It was about 8:30 PM. I leaned on my staff. Suddenly there was a wave from the front. People in line were sitting down on the sidewalk. Everyone sat down in their place in line. When the wave got to us, Kirsten and Wolf sat down, but I remained standing, leaning on my staff. Almost at the same time as this, a big bald man in a grey T-shirt walked around the corner of the building from the front. He spotted me leaning on my staff and walked quickly toward me.

"What are you doing out here?" He asked. "We've been waiting for you to show. Come on, let's go in." Kirsten and Wolf stood up and we moved toward the entrance. We could feel the stares of the people in line. Kirsten looked like she felt a little smug, but I felt guilty to be cutting all these people in line. We had made it almost to the entrance when I heard a girl's voice.

"Hey! HEY!" I turned my head. It was Cindy from the first night I had seen the Dugouts back in ------. She was with a mixed group of guys and girls. She kind of put her weight forward on one leg which made her hip sway out. "You could get us in too couldn't you?" I looked at her. She was as stunning as ever.

I looked at the man who was getting us in. "Not all of them," he said. "Maybe her by herself." I looked at her and told her what the man had said. She looked at her

119

friends, especially the boy she was standing with. She kissed him on the cheek, but then walked, swaying again, over to us. I don't know why I had even stopped to listen to her. I barely knew her. I guess there's a reason. We continued our way into the warehouse, with Cindy alongside us. I looked at Kirsten for the first time, and she didn't look very happy. There were other big guys wearing grey shirts at the front door, and they opened the doors for us. This time, I was prepared for something special.

*   *   *   *   *

We walked into darkness. The shapes of the crowd were indistinct, but the warehouse was packed full. The stage was dark as well, but there was a humming noise coming from it. The big bald man abandoned us to make his way along the side of the warehouse walls. There was no real chance of us getting much closer at this point, but it appeared that we would be able to see the stage. Then, from the darkness, a voice emerged from the hum. The crowd grew quiet.

"The masters have spoken, the end is near. Never have we had so much to fear. The dead awake with staring eyes. Kill and destroy, they multiply. Hope has come from near and far. The forest sings up to the stars. The scene begins on Dark Continent. That is where we shall be sent. Why is it our time to live? Why is it our time to die? Why is the wait so long? Why is the wait so hard? IT'S TIME TO STRIKE!"

And the red lights came up, and the band was already on stage. They started to play immediately. The crowd yelled and applauded. The Dugouts were leaning over at the waist, and nodding their heads in time to the beat. It was throbbing, and loud, louder than I'd ever heard them before. Almost immediately, large white flashbulbs went off in a row, from one side of the stage to the other, and back again. Robbins sang of love and death, and the path between. The crowd was jumping up and down in place. Cindy yelled and shouted with the rest of them. Kirsten was standing next to Wolf and rubbing his fur. Wolf's tail was down as if he felt slightly out of place.

The Dugouts played for awhile, and then stopped. The next song came on, and it was obviously a crowd favorite. Some people were singing every word, and a large circle formed in the center of the warehouse. It didn't seem like there would be any room between people, but there was room in the circle for people to run around, and run they did. They were bumping into each other and the people at the edges of the circle, using their shoulders and forearms. Even outside the circle, people were jostling and being crushed. Slowly, against my will, I was pushed closer to the circle. Both of my hands were on the staff, so it was hard to avoid it. I got pushed into the actual circle itself, and people were slamming into me, pushing me every which way. If not for the lights of the stage flashing by me every few seconds, I would have completely lost my bearings. Then someone's hands were on the staff, trying to pull it away from me. I held on for dear life, still being pounded by others. Then there was a growling, and a large black blur jumped on the man trying to steal the staff. He fell away from me, with Wolf straddling his form. The circle shrunk again, and people were just milling about inside it. The song was over, and there was some applause, but it wasn't overwhelming as before.

"Let him up, Wolf," I said. Wolf let the man get to his feet. He was a large man, with tattoos on his arms. Men in grey T-shirts fought through the crowd to get to him, and they grabbed him by the arms. The man with tattoos looked at us with hatred as they escorted him to the front door. Kirsten and Cindy fought their way through the crowd to us as a new song started.

Kirsten yelled to me over the music. "That man tried to steal the staff! Did you know him?" I shrugged helplessly, conveying my ignorance. People were starting to get into the music again. The lights had turned from red to green and white. Robbins was singing of the impossibility of a journey between the stars, and why an alien intelligence had never come to Earth. The bass player, Danno, was providing the melody to the song, and a beat that skipped around normal time signatures. The lead guitar played notes that wailed and dived, seemingly unrelated, but somehow fitting in.

Cindy turned to me and spoke in my ear. "Thanks for getting me in. I've been dying to see these guys again. My friends here in New York said they were playing and I couldn't stay away." Something about her had changed. She was still beautiful, but she no longer seemed as cool and detached as she had been.

Kirsten butted in. "We're on an important mission here. It's not just about seeing the band, you know." My eyes were still glued to the stage. Robbins started at one side of the stage and waved a towel around his head in the air. The people on that side of the stage went crazy, and he walked across the stage, waving the towel, and people went crazy in front of him.

They played a few more songs. Then Robbins stood in front with the drummer playing a march. "The evil has reached deep into Africa," he said. "The government will do nothing to stop the killing. We must go and fight the battle before the cancer spreads to the whole world. We're chartering a private flight to go to Africa. The flight will have a supply of weapons. The guys at the door will hand out your tickets if you will go. The flight leaves JFK tomorrow. Please come to save Africa and, in so doing, save the United States. Please leave now and get your tickets so others may be recruited."

With that, the lights in the warehouse came on, and everyone was looking at each other with a puzzled expression. The show had hardly begun before it was over. "Please!" Robbins reiterated. "Meet us tomorrow at JFK. Make room for the people that are waiting outside." The crowd began moving sullenly to the doors. Most of them took tickets as they went. As we started to go, the big bald man in the grey T-shirt stopped us. "No, you guys go backstage," he said. "We'll take you to the airport tomorrow." We followed him around the side of the stage to a back room. We had to pass several large men in grey T-shirts to get there. The band was lounging around on couches. There were others standing and talking, or passing joints around. There was a table laid out with sandwiches and hors d'oeuvres. Some people were drinking beer from a keg that was in a garbage can with ice. Cindy was in her element, immediately attracting a great deal of attention in the room. She passed from group to group, talking animatedly. Wolf looked up at me and then looked at the sandwiches. I took the meat out of a couple of sandwiches and fed it to him.

Robbins came over to us while I was feeding Wolf. "It is a big break for us that you have the staff," he said. "Have you really destroyed the Borzhat crystals with it?"

"Yes, that's true," I said, a little unhappily.

"Hopefully, that ability will be useful in our coming battle in Africa. You will come, right?"

"I don't suppose we have any choice," I said. "That seems to be the way things are headed." Cindy had her beer and made her way back to us now that Robbins was there.

Kirsten spoke up. "We'll be glad to help. It's the same fight on all these different worlds, and I've always wanted to be a part of it."

Cindy spoke to Robbins. "I want to help too. I'm sure I can fight with these guys."

Kirsten replied. "This isn't a party we're going to. You might break a nail."

Robbins held up his hands. "Anyone can help, Okay? We need everyone we can get." He turned around and went back to the couch where his little group had been sitting. Kirsten went over to Wolf at the sandwich table. He was still looking hungry, and she fed him some more meat from the sandwiches.

Cindy leaned over to me and whispered in my ear. "There's a ladder to the roof," she said. "Do you want to go up?" I nodded, looking back at Kirsten for some reason. Cindy led the way around a corner and started climbing the ladder. She was wearing a mid-length skirt, and I could see her beautiful legs as she climbed. I climbed after her. We walked around the roof, which didn't seem very stable. We leaned over the side and saw the line around the warehouse moving slowly as people entered the building. We couldn't see much of New York because most of the buildings were too tall to see over.

Cindy took my hand and we sat down. "Can I see the staff?" I complied, and she made the usual noises about how impressive the carvings were. "I didn't know The Dugouts were connected to some larger battle," she said. "I just knew it was a special movement. You missed a good wish party by the way."

I was nonplussed. "What is a wish party anyway?"

Cindy gave me a coy smile. "A wish party is a party where all your wishes come true for as long as the party lasts. They're fun, but very addictive. It can be hard to come back to reality sometimes. You know, I've been feeling sad about my life. It seems like I've done everything there is to do. It seems like I've seen everything there is to see. That's why I was trying to follow the Dugouts. They've brought me more excitement than anything I've ever done in my life."

I looked at her carefully. "I think feeling like you've done everything comes with age. As you grow older, you really have done more things, and it takes more to excite you."

"Well I'm not very old," she said. "I hope this feeling doesn't get worse as time goes on. I'll be ready to commit suicide before I'm fifty." Just then the full moon came out from behind a cloud. "Isn't that beautiful?" she asked. "You know women know more about the moon than men do."

"I can believe that," I said. "The moon is mysterious

and ever changing, kind of like women."

"Yes, we are mysterious," she replied. "I'm starting to think you know something about women."

"I know something about the moon," I said. "The same part of the moon always faces earth. It rotates about perfectly so we never see the other side of the moon."

"Really?" she said. "That's interesting. There must be some kind of explanation for that." Suddenly there was a loud crash of music. The Dugouts had started playing again. Cindy kissed me quickly but firmly on the lips and said, "Let's go back down. We can probably hear better from backstage." I was a little surprised by the kiss but followed her wordlessly back down the ladder.

The backstage area was mostly empty when we returned, but Kirsten was there with Wolf. They came up to us, and Kirsten spoke. "Hey, tell me when you're going to go off somewhere. I was worried."

Cindy smirked. "You're not our keeper. We can go wherever we want."

Kirsten replied. "Maybe so, but the staff is the most important thing. If we lose that, we lose everything. Please be careful."

I felt my responsibility again and turned to Cindy. "It's true," I said. "We should have told her we were leaving. We do have a responsibility to this movement."

Cindy looked at me. "Well, I'm going to go watch the band." She flounced out of the room. Wolf rubbed his head against my waist. I needed a pick me up right then, and I scratched him behind the ears.

"Why did you invite her in with us?" Kirsten asked. "She doesn't really believe in what we're doing. Do you even know her?"

I replied. "I know her now. She wants to help, that's all."

"You don't think she has an ulterior motive?"

"What ulterior motive? Now you're just being paranoid. Just relax now. We'll be in Africa soon enough with plenty to do."

Kirsten looked a little mollified and completed the conversation. "Okay, I suppose you're right. We need all the help we can get." I wondered whether I should drink a beer. I hadn't had a drink in a long time, but I felt the need to relax. I decided to get one from the keg. I could hear the music loudly, but I couldn't tell exactly what Robbins was singing about. The beer tasted good all the way to my stomach. It was almost a panacea. I sat down on one of the couches. Kirsten came over and sat down next to me. She leaned her head on my arm. Wolf came over and lay down on my feet.

I suddenly realized that I wasn't alone anymore. For years I had been traveling from place to place, switching jobs. I never had any friends, and I was never invited in to any groups. But now, I was surrounded by people that stayed with me all the time. Wolf was here, the one I had saved. Now he had saved me from the Borzhat. He was my companion, loyal and true. He never asked questions, or talked much for that matter, but I could depend on him. Kirsten was also here. She was a fiery willful redhead, dedicated to the cause, and she always had good ideas. It all just added to the way I was fond of her. A sudden feeling of contentment came over me. Even though I was unsure of the future, I was happy right now. That's what's important, really.

After about an hour, the band finished a set, and repeated their plea to the crowd to join them in going to Africa. The crowd seemed a little more excited this time, and we could hear them discussing things as they left the warehouse. The backstage area filled up again, and Cindy came back. She went immediately to get a beer. The band came back too, and Danno came over to us. "This is going fairly well, I think. We've had other concerts in other locations and told people about the issue. Africa will never know what hit it!"

I looked up at him. "We're going to have to find a hotel or something. We've got no place to stay."

Danno made a reproachful gesture. "Not at all, you can stay here. We've got sleeping pads for the trip to Africa. You can use them and sleep on the floor. A lot of people are doing it."

The backstage party continued into the night, but we took the pads and went out into the warehouse and crashed. We'd had a long day walking around in New York, and we were tired. Cindy partied into the night, but eventually joined us, putting her pad next to mine and waking me for a time. We were all ready for the trip to Africa the next day.

❖ Chapter 9

"To the memory of the Man, first in war, first in peace, and first in the hearts of his countrymen."

Henry Lee, Memoirs of Lee. Eulogy on Washington

The next day, I awoke with my arms wrapped around Cindy, clinging close. I immediately disengaged, but Cindy awoke with my movement. She turned and smiled at me, and then blinked her eyes in a fetching manner. At that moment, Danno came into the large area of the warehouse and woke us all up.

"Up and at 'em, everybody. The planes leave in a few hours, and we want to be there early to greet the others." Everybody started stirring, and I looked over at Kirsten. She was already up, leaning on her elbow looking at me. I wondered how much she had seen. Wolf got to his feet and yawned hugely. We did the usual morning things and then prepared to leave for JFK. Danno guided us all to the right subways, and we took the trains to the edge of Queens. Once we got to the airport, we went to a gate reserved for private charters and looked at our plane. There was a large plane sitting waiting for us, and we all felt a sense of accomplishment. The Dugouts were slapping each other on the back and looking excited. A few people began to show up, and were assigned buddies and a seat. However, as the time drew near to leave, it became obvious that not many people were coming to Africa with us. There was the awkward feeling that you have at the beginning of a party where you don't know if people are going to show up yet. Then you wait and wait, and know that hardly anyone is going to come, and it's not going to be one of those parties, the great parties. It won't be a party where people meet new interesting people, and maybe fall in love. Well, this feeling was coming to the Dugouts, and I don't think it was a feeling they were used to. There were only fifty people milling around the tarmac, and the plane had room for several hundred easily.

The Dugouts waited past the time when people were supposed to arrive, and the others waited mostly silently. Eventually Robbins told us all to get on the plane.

"We may need the extra room," he said. "We may have to evacuate people from Kenya. That's our destination, Nairobi!" Everyone piled onto the plane, and we took off.

The flight was interminable. It's horrible to be stuck in one place, without being able to freely roam around. Even though it was a chartered flight, and there were no particular rules for staying in our seats, there was really nowhere to go. Danno took some time explaining what we would be given. We would all have packs with basic camping items. We would all be given guns and machetes. We would stay the first night in Nairobi, and then make our way to a more remote village in the Rift Valley. We would discover what was happening in the village and try to defeat the enemy, and come back to America with our story of what should be done in Africa.

Eventually, we landed at the NBO. There was a private gate reserved for us, and the safari equipment was loaded onto a truck. We were all to meet at the Holiday Inn Nairobi and stay the night there. We had a little time before we were supposed to meet, so Cindy, Kirsten, Wolf, and I did some sight-seeing. We went to the Kenyan

National Museum. It was a two story structure, and we spent most of our time on the second floor, looking at the stuffed animals, and tribal displays. It was mostly empty.

When we went back into the city to go to the hotel, we noticed a tense atmosphere. Everyone was hurrying to their destinations without looking around. There was no laughter on the street corners. No one was just hanging around. It was almost a sense of panic. We got back to the hotel, and it was early evening. We decided to eat in the hotel restaurant, even though that's not supportive of independent restaurant owners. We all knew we were to meet in the morning to go to our village. It was a Masai village, a popular culture for tourists, but still a true African people. After dinner we went up to our rooms. Wolf and I had a room, while Kirsten and Cindy had a room of their own. I wasn't sure how good an idea that was, but that was the way the buddy system works. In our rooms were our packs for the trip. Only Wolf did not have a pack. I had a dangerous looking semi-automatic weapon that I had no idea how to use. I didn't even know what kind it was, or if it was perhaps fully automatic. As far as I could tell, it wasn't loaded, so I wasn't going to shoot Wolf by accident. Kirsten and Cindy dropped by the room after a little while.

"Did you see the guns they gave us?" Cindy asked. "I hope we don't have to use them."

Kirsten replied, "We probably will have to use them. We are going into battle, after all."

Wolf spoke. "Everyone smells of fear here. Something is not right."

Even I had picked up on the nervousness around Nairobi. "We'll get to the bottom of things tomorrow,"

I said. "What do you want to do tonight, until we go to bed?"

Cindy piped up quickly. "We could play 'Never have I ever' with the beer in the refrigerators."

Kirsten replied. "That's a stupid idea. This is serious business."

Cindy protested. "No, it'll be fun. It will be a way to get to know each other better."

"I'll play," I said. "I could use a beer."

Cindy went to Wolf and scratched his head. "You'll play, won't you Wolf? I want to learn about you." Wolf wagged his tail, but didn't say anything.

"Great!" Cindy said. "That's three. Come on Kirsten, you're the only hold out."

"All right," Kirsten sighed. "Whatever you want." Cindy jumped up and got the beers as we positioned ourselves on the beds across from each other. Wolf sat on the floor with a dish for his beer.

I spoke to Cindy. "Refresh us on the rules of this game. I'm a little rusty."

"Okay," Cindy said. "You say, "Never have I ever" and then say something that you've done or haven't done. If you've done it, you have to drink, and so does anybody else that's done it. We take turns saying things about ourselves. I'll start. Never have I ever seen T he Dugouts play live. I think everyone has to drink on that one." We all drank a sip of beer.

I was sitting to her left, so I went next. "Never have I ever, uh let's see, been to Africa before this trip." No one drank. Wolf was next in line.

"Never eaten corn." I laughed at that, and we all

133

drank except for Wolf. Kirsten was next.

"Never have I ever slept with someone after just meeting them." I had to drink, but so did Cindy. Cindy frowned.

"That was mean! Oh well, Never have I ever taken a mind-altering substance." She drank again, and so did I. Kirsten drank too. Cindy looked pleased with herself. "Ah, I got you back," she said.

It was my turn. "Never have I ever eaten raw red meat," I said. I was determined to get Wolf back for the corn. He drank obligingly and went next.

"Never broken Borzhat crystal." I growled at him and drank. Cindy drank too.

Kirsten flared up. "You never!"

Cindy giggled. "I know. I just wanted a sip of beer." Kirsten put down her beer.

"I'm not playing anymore. I'm going to bed." She flounced out of the room. She probably would have slammed the door if they weren't soft-closing doors.

Cindy looked at me. "Well, I guess it's just us now." For some reason, I wasn't in the mood anymore.

"I think I'm going to go to bed, Cindy," I said. "It's getting late, and I'm sure we have a long day tomorrow."

"Well fine!" She said, and drank the rest of her beer in one swig. She flounced out of the room almost identically to Kirsten. I wondered what the other room would be like with the two of them in bad moods. Soon, though, I just got ready for bed. While I was getting ready, I turned on the TV. There were scenes of empty villages, burned villages. Everywhere there was carnage, but there were no views of dead people. The people seemed to have disappeared. I changed to one channel, and there was a view of people dancing in a circle to drums. They had paint on their faces and chests. Some had gruesome and disfiguring scars. They leered at the camera and laughed. There was one dark man who had hair in a large afro. He bowed to the camera and smiled hugely. He did a dance waving his fat belly around while he stamped his foot on the ground. Then he reached to the sky, and looked up above his weaving arms. It was all somewhat threatening, and I soon turned the TV off to go to bed.

* * * * *

The next day, The Dugouts were rounding everyone up to meet in the lobby. There was the usual chaos associated with this kind of meeting. Everyone was talking in groups as things were organized. Eventually we were all loaded on to buses to head out of the city. Sitting next to us on our bus were a black-clad couple. They had black jeans on and black T-shirts. They were both very pale, but it was their natural skin tone, they seemed quite self-possessed. The guy had a silver cross around his neck. They were staying to themselves, but Cindy was sitting next to them, and she has a way of meeting people. We found out that they had lived last in Dallas, but that they always had to move to look for work. Pretty soon they were talking about how it seemed that The Dugouts were playing in every city they moved to. It almost seemed as if The Dugouts were following them around. So they had decided to go to New York to see the special concert and go to Africa on this trip. The man's name was Devon, and the woman's name was April. She didn't talk very much, but had a delicate composure that was somewhat enticing.

We talked off and on for hours as the bus left the city and headed out into the country. We pulled off onto a side road, and traveled for a ways off the beaten path. Danno stood up in the front of the bus and spoke.

"We're headed up to a shooting range here. All of you will learn how to use your guns so we can fight the danger that is threatening Africa." Soon we did indeed arrive at a shooting range, and we exited the buses. We gathered around the shooting range with our guns. Thankfully, no one had loaded up, or someone might have gotten shot in the chaos. We split up into groups. Danno headed up our group, which included our party, Devon and April, and a couple of others that we didn't know. Danno began speaking.

"First and foremost, never point your gun at someone, unless you intend to shoot them. You never know when it could accidentally go off. Pointing the gun in the air is generally a good practice when you're hiking, which we may be doing a good deal of. Stay even with each other so no one gets ahead and gets mistaken for the enemy. We may have to go single file, in which case you can point your gun off to the side. When you engage the enemy, move in groups and take cover. Do NOT get separated. That is the easiest way to shoot each other. The way to use these guns is fairly simple. You put the magazine with the bullets in, pull back on the slide, and you're ready to shoot. There's a vertical hand grip you should use when you're firing, and a laser scope for long distance shooting. The hand grip has a flashlight on it so if it's night you can use that. Don't give away your position with it though. Okay, I think we're ready to take some practice rounds at the targets. Just line up, and begin when ready."

We readied our weapons and lined up at the targets. The gun felt heavy in my hands, as if it was reluctant to begin. I figured out how to turn the laser scope on, and aimed at a bull's eye target. I squeezed the trigger, and the gun jumped in my hands. I guessed that I had missed high. I hadn't hit the target at all. I held the gun firmly for the next shot, and hit near the center. Once I was holding the gun firmly, it seemed lighter, ready for action. I fired several more times, and then stopped to see how my companions were doing. Devon had used guns before and hit a good grouping near the center. Kirsten and Cindy were having problems with the recoil however. Kirsten eventually was hitting the target with some regularity, but Cindy never got it. Kirsten's shots seemed to be going to the left. After a half-hour and some clips, we ran through a short course in groups. We used rented paintball guns, but everyone was still pretty excited after it was over. Many looked worried that it might come to actual action. At the same time, people were tired in a good way from the rush of adrenaline. We made our way back to the buses.

After we were back on the main road the mood was quiet. We stared out the windows into a plain dotted with trees. Strange and disinterested animals would pass by us. Soon, the plain gave way to a real forest. Unfamiliar trees crowded the road as the buses bumped along the uneven roads. For awhile, watching the forest passed the time quickly, but it was all the same strangeness. Even the animals ceased to entertain as the bus ride lengthened into hours. The forest went on unceasingly as the terrain roughened. Eventually, the trees thinned out into a plain.

The transition to the plain made things even less interesting, and Devon turned to me to begin a story.

"Before we moved to Dallas, we were living in a small town outside of Austin. There was little to do there but go to a corporate coffeehouse that had set up on the nice side of town. April and I tried to meet people, but most were living their own lives, and didn't seem interested in sharing their time with us. April worked in a diner, but I was unable to find a job doing anything, as there was very little going on in the town. One night I was picking April up from work after a lunch shift, and a man dressed in leather approached me as I got out of my car. He was a biker, and he asked me for gas money to get to Austin. He said he was going to a fantastic show that some other bikers were going to, but he was down on his luck and out of money. I asked him about the show, and he told me that it was a band called The Dugouts. April and I had seen The Dugouts several times already, and I was excited that they were playing so close to us. April joined us after she was done with her shift, and we decided to go with him. We gave him twenty dollars for gas, and got on the highway. It was about a two hour drive to Austin, and the biker wanted to haul ass, but we had already told him to go a speed that our beat up Civic could handle.

"We got into Austin and crossed these railroad tracks into a warehouse district. There was a biker working the door of our destination, and he let us in for free after a short conversation with the man we had helped. After we got inside, the biker slipped me a green and red herb and said that he had to hang with his friends for the rest of the night, and couldn't stay with us. That was fine with me and

138

April, and we went over to a makeshift bar along the side of the warehouse. We chewed up the herb between us and waited for the band to begin. April was so happy that we were finally getting to do something for once, and her eyes were shining in the dim room. Eventually, the drummer came out and sat down at the drums. He kicked the bass drum with a steady beat as the crowd roared. He played around with the cymbals a little, and then moved to the snare and toms. All the while he was keeping a steady beat on the bass drum. Slowly at first, but then more and more, the floor began to vibrate in time to the drum. The concrete seemed to become slippery in time to the vibrations, and we slid around unintentionally in time to the music.

"Then the bass player came on stage, and he started playing a note up high on the bass when the drum thumped. Each time he played a high note, he slid it down to a lower note. It seemed a slippery counterpoint to the floor. Then the guitar player came on stage, and when he started playing wailing notes on his guitar, a wind seemed to blow from the stage, cooling the hot room. At first the wind was a steady blast, but then it swirled and eddied, as it seemed to follow his diving swoops on the fret board.

"Finally, Robbins came out wearing a dark trenchcoat. He grabbed the mic with his left hand and stretched out an open hand toward the audience. The crowd roared again. He began singing low notes, and tendrils of darkness seemed to blow around his frame into the audience. The darkness flowed from around his hand like water, and swirled into the crowd. The darkness entered some peoples eyes, and their pupils dilated until there was nothing but black in their eyes. Then their clothing seemed to thicken and take on length until they were wearing trenchcoats as well. Lines of straight white light began to shoot across the ceiling, making speedy right angled turns. The lines moved so quickly that a reddish afterimage was left after they passed. There seemed to be some mathematical purpose to the whole sequence, but it was unfathomable. Robbins began yelling out numbers. '37, 24, 81!' I don't remember the numbers now, but they seemed important somehow at the time. The opening song ended.

"Then with a crash, the band began a new song. The white lights on the ceiling continued unabated, and behind the band a large misty blue globe began to coalesce. Soon it was evident that it was a globe of the earth. It rotated slowly and gave off a pale blue light. Then it seemed that water was pouring from the bottom of the earth on to the stage. The water spilled out between the band members onto the warehouse floor. The water began to accumulate. The water covered our ankles, and then our knees. The water level rose up to our waist, and then our armpits. I saw April's head go under water. I panicked, diving under the water to be near her, but she seemed to be breathing just fine. I looked up at the stage again, and the globe was mostly brown now, the oceans gone. As the water enveloped me, the noise from the band became distorted, but louder. April's hair swirled around her as the turbulent water rose to fill the room. Soon, everyone was floating just under the ceiling of the warehouse. The bright lines of light that were criss-crossing the ceiling began to dive straight down into the water. They hissed as they struck the water, and then dropped straight down to the floor. A trail of tiny bubbles followed them as they plunged through the dimly lit water. The lights seemed to avoid people somehow, but occasionally struck one of the newly trenchcoated fans. For a moment, it appeared as if the trenchcoated figure was hung from a straight line of light. The man or woman in the trenchcoat would be frozen in time. It would happen only for a moment, and then the trenchcoated figure could move again.

"April and I became separated once, and when we found each other, we held hands so that we would not be lost under water. The band continued to play songs to grab your attention and hold it. At one point they became quieter, and the water began to subside. But it did so in a strange way. A thin pocket of air appeared on the floor and grew larger. The water appeared to flow into the ceiling somehow. Perhaps it was draining into the sky through the vents. Or perhaps it was just flowing back onto the earth globe on the stage. It was hard to tell in the confusion of being underwater. We dropped out of the water to land slowly and softly on the concrete floor. Pretty soon the water was all gone, and steam was rising from everyone in the close quarters. Robbins doffed his trenchcoat to reveal a black T-shirt. The band played on into the night, but most of the strangeness was over. We were tired, but made the drive back home. That concert was one of the real special ones. It was a time when you feel invincible, like nothing can go wrong. We'd seen concerts before, and we've seen concerts after that one, but that's the one that will always stick out in our minds."

Devon seemed to have said his piece. He sat back in his seat with a sigh. We were still riding through the plains of Kenya. Mountains surrounded us in the distance. We gassed up on the outskirts of the city of Eldoret and stopped to eat. We picked up some guides that spoke the local languages, and tried to make our target village before it was too late at night. If anything, the locals at Eldoret were even more nervous than the ones in Nairobi. They looked at us with suspicion. It encouraged us to get on the busses and head for our village. The buses rode slowly through Eldoret; the empty markets, the hostile stares. Soon we were out in the country again, riding through plains. Danno said our destination was only a half hour away. It was to be a little village called Humori.

After a short time on the road, we pulled into a small village. The Masai people came out of their dwellings in celebration, raising their arms and yelling. Children were dancing around the buses. The town had been forewarned of our arrival and was expecting us. As we departed the bus with our packs, the villagers surrounded us, dancing and laughing. We gathered together among the throng, and a tall man with short grey hair approached. The crowd quieted and he spoke loudly in broken English.

"Welcome to our saviors. Welcome to those who would fight the evil that surrounds us. Our hopes lie with you this day!" As he finished, the crowd shouted again, but began to disperse. A few of the villagers led us to a place on the outskirts of town where we would be able to set up our tents. Kirsten picked a spot right away and began putting her poles together. Cindy dumped her tent on the ground, and then looked at me helplessly.

I sighed. "I'll help you put up your tent after I get mine up," I said. I picked a spot, but there was a large black bird in the way. It had a long tapered beak that came to a point with a red turkey beard and a red pointed patch around its eye. A guide was nearby, and I asked him what it was. He replied, "Hornbill," and continued on about his business. The guides were actually fairly dedicated to the cause, but they were very busy with people asking for water and bathrooms and such. I finished setting up my tent, and turned to Cindy. She smiled at me winningly, and Kirsten rolled her eyes. But just then, Danno came up to us. He pointed at me and Wolf.

"Please come with me to the Elders dwelling," he said. I looked at Cindy's tent, and Kirsten groaned. "I'll put it up, don't worry about it." Wolf and I followed Danno into the center of the village. At length, we came to a mud house larger than the others, with a red tapestry hanging over the door. I waited for Danno to go in, but he shook his head and motioned me inside. I pushed aside the curtain and entered, with Wolf close at my heels. I entered a long room lit by some kind of camping lanterns. A group of old villagers was seated in a semicircle in the middle of the room. Closing the semicircle on our side was Robbins, the drummer from the band, and two other men I had seen working with the band as security. Aside from Robbins, all were big and heavily muscled. The drummer was not wearing a shirt, and he had a tattoo of a vine growing out of a skull with jewels for teeth. The skull was on his arm, and the vines crossed over his chest and sprouted flowers on his neck. They all looked at me, and then went back to talking with one of the guides. Apart from me and Wolf, the guide was the only one standing. We took our places in the circle.

The man with the grey hair that welcomed us was there, and he spoke. "I think we can begin. I know you are here to help us. This is the news of our area. Whole villages are being destroyed. The homes are wrecked and burned. The people mysteriously disappear. And our hunters find signs of large groups of people making trails through the woods. It is as if there is a large army living in the forest, destroying towns and recruiting the villagers. There are signs of resistance, blood and empty shells. But no bodies are ever found! It is good that you got here when you did. We worry that the army is ready to move against our village. We have no real means of defending ourselves." He finished, and the villagers nodded agreement.

Robbins responded, and the guide translated his words. "We bring many dedicated people to your cause. We have many guns, and supplies for a long stay. We know we may be fighting a strong and ruthless enemy, but we are ready to lay down our lives to protect your village. If it becomes necessary, there is room on the buses for some of your children to escape. We had thought to bring even more people, but complacency in America is more the rule than not. Still, even with our diminished numbers, I believe we are prepared." As the guide translated that, an old woman sitting on the other side of the circle coughed and leaned forward. I looked down at her wrap, which was a dark red and covered with white words I could not understand. She glanced at me and spoke directly to me. The guide translated.

"You like my Kanga apron? It was my grandmother's. It says, 'The trees rise to cover me with their cooling shade. The rivers run to cool me with their covering waters. Water brings life to all of the earth, and I feel the water of the earth flow through my life.' You know how to bring the love of the earth here to fight this evil. You are our greatest hope. The man with the great dog. It is said that the time for the ultimate answer draws near. You must prevent this. Of all our enemies here facing us, it is said there is a prime enemy. Some child has seen him and told me of him. He is large, and has a blue jewel embedded in his forehead where his third eye should be. He must be the leader of this evil army that is growing stronger every day." The woman coughed again and fell silent.

The tall man with the grey hair spoke again. "We will give you four of our hunters to help you find the enemy. Other than that, we have little help for you from this village. As long as we are here there will be food, water, and that camping ground for you. Is there anything that we can provide that you require?"

Robbins put his hands flat on soil and then dusted them off on his pants. "No, we will start in the morning. Hopefully, we can protect this one village from harm. Thank you for your hospitality." Everyone stood at that, and some began talking with each other. Fairly quickly, the delegation from our side left for the camping area. Robbins was in the lead, and he gestured for us to follow him. He led us to a large tent that was open on all sides except for mosquito netting. Some others joined us who had not been in the village meeting. There was a small camping table set up that we gathered around.

Robbins began by spreading out a map. "This is an accurate contour map of the area. The hunters tell us that the opposing army is in this forest valley here. Our plan is a simple one. The bulk of our forces will try to keep them from coming through the valley mouth toward the village. We should have enough firepower to accomplish this task for days. A small group will circle around and come in from the rear and try to kill their leader. If we destroy the crystal in his head, their forces will all collapse, and perhaps the threat to Africa will be over. We can only hope that he is the only leader, and that no others exist. The only question should be about how small the group should be."

One of the men in a grey shirt responded. "It should be ten people, all male. They will be able to move faster around the rim of the valley. Hopefully ten will be enough to attack the leadership without weakening our blockading forces."

Danno questioned this. "Do we need to split up our forces at all? We are too few as it is. Maybe we should all circle around to the other side of the valley and attack the enemy."

The drummer responded. "We have made a commitment to this village. We can't just flush the enemy forward into the village. We have radios with a fairly long range. We should be able to keep in touch if anything goes wrong."

Robbins spoke. "Okay, the man and the Wolf, you Jericho, you Davies," he gestured toward the drummer and one of the bouncers. "Take two of the hunters with you. Pick four more from the group that came with us. Make one of them the radio guy. No girls. You'll have to move fast. I guess you should take the map. We'll make do with the locals. Is that all right with everyone?" He paused for a few seconds. "Well then, in the morning we move out."

Jericho and Davies started to make the rounds of the camp to find a few more for our mission. I went back to my tent with Wolf. Cindy and Kirsten were there waiting for me, as well as Devon and April.

Kirsten spoke first. "Well? What's the plan? What did they want you for?" I told them the gist of the plan and Devon exclaimed. "I want to go too. I can carry the radio and help out." He set off immediately to find Jericho and Davies.

Kirsten continued. "No girls? That's not fair! They mean to split us up?" I had no real reply to this, and I looked at Cindy. She looked uncomfortable too, as she realized she would be part of a blockade action. It was already fairly late however, and we decided to turn in. Wolf lay down outside my tent, and I tried to get comfortable. It was far too hot out here in the open. Eventually I fell asleep, and as I slept I dreamed.

❖ Chapter 10

"Wine is wont to show the mind of man."
Theognis, Maxims

All was darkness. How do you know you are dreaming when there are no visions to tell you? But there was sound eventually. A constant drumming. Not a joyful sound, but more of a tortured rhythm. It was like that old fairy tale of the girl who puts on the magical shoes that make her dance until she drops dead from exhaustion. The sound that the shoes would make was like the drumming I heard in my dream. I ventured nearer through the jungle, pushing the dark branches and large leaves away from my face. The drumming grew louder and wilder. Soon, I could see the drummers in a clearing. Instead of sitting in a circle, they were lined up in rows. It was almost a military formation. Half-naked people danced crazily in front of the drummers. Most had horrible scars, and were painted with black paint. Suddenly a voice spoke from beside me.

"They are always like this before war," it said. "They whip themselves into a frenzy." The voice came from a huge man. The musculature of his body was squared off, and doughy. It looked inhuman. His eyes were only whites, as if he'd been blind since birth, and there was a blue jewel embedded in the center of his forehead. His hair was white, and he was pale, like an albino. "I can sense that you are near," he said. "Do you plan to stop me here?" I could not speak. "It does not matter. You are too late. You will never be able to stop the spread of the Borzhat." I was still mute, unable to speak. I wanted to banter with him, perhaps get him to spill some information, but I was silent, struggling. "Let me tell you of a wondrous place," he said. "It has caves of lava and fire. The caves burrow deep into the earth. In the very center of a mountain lies the great lava lake. A thin bridge crosses this lake, and it leads to the Temple of Kreaco-Ath. This is where I was born. Three high-priests of the Borzhat were my fathers, each more powerful than you can imagine. They use the Primus Crystal to spread fear and destruction. They created me to destroy this world. Now bring the staff to me," he said. "I will break it and break you." He moved closer, and his face filled my vision. The drumming grew even wilder if possible. "You are weak. You do not truly love the world you live on. What have you done for it? Nothing! You continue to do nothing! You are nothing!" All I could see were his eyes and the crystal. Pure white orbs and an evil shining light. I felt his will as if it was a physical pressure, but I was waking up then.

The afterimage of his eyes and crystal faded slowly, and I was left with a headache. The morning was cooler, and the headache faded, but the dream had shaken me. There were large spiders all over the mesh of my tent, and I called to Wolf.

"Hey, Wolf. Look out for these spiders." He raised his head and looked at the tent. He stood up and moved a distance away. I started flicking the spiders off the tent with my finger, away from Wolf's direction.

He circled and came back. "No other tents have spiders," he said. They were crawling out of sight. I unzipped the door to my tent and got out. We were among the first to awaken, but Cindy was also awake.

She approached my tent with an inscrutable expression on her face. She stopped in front of me. "I don't want you to go with the others. I don't want to separate," she said meaningfully.

I was at a loss. "I have to go," I said. "The mission depends on me being able to destroy the crystal in that creature's head. I don't like splitting up the group either, but that was what was decided."

Cindy looked at me carefully, and then put her hands to the sides of my face. "I wouldn't have come if it wasn't for you," she said. Then she kissed me carefully on the lips. I hesitated at first, but then put my arms around her and returned the kiss. She was so attractive, and I had never seen a side to her that was vulnerable. We broke apart by mutual consent, as if we didn't want to start anything more.

"I have to meet the others," I said. "I'm sure they are already beginning to gather." I pulled the staff from out of my tent, and started tearing down my campsite.

Devon came up to me and started talking as I continued to pack up. "I'm on the team," he said. "We're leaving soon from the main tent. Then we'll double time it to the ridge with the hunters." He stayed with me while I finished up. Cindy stayed off to the side.

Soon, Kirsten crawled out of her tent as well. Her hair was tousled, and she looked tired. "I guess this is goodbye," she said. "I hope we'll see each other again, but who knows what will happen in this battle." Wolf came up next to her and bumped against her and looked up into her eyes. I walked over to her as well and gave her a big hug. She leaned up and whispered into my ear. "Please be careful, something about this feels wrong." April said her goodbyes to Devon, and the three girls stood by the empty clearing where my tent had been as Devon, Wolf, and I walked to the big tent. The drummer Jericho was there, as was the bouncer Davies.

Robbins was there, but he was busy with others, and he only stopped for a moment to talk to us. "Good luck gentlemen," he said. "You know what to do. Make all possible speed you can." He turned back to a swarm of grey-shirted men that were demanding his attention. It turned out that Devon was going to carry the radio. It also turned out that several of the ten of us had too much in our packs, so we lightened up. We were going to double up in tents, so that took some weight off of our shoulders. We carried our guns out with the safeties on, and once that was decided, we were on our way.

We took one of the busses as far down a road as we could, but the road ran out soon. We exited the bus and jogged at a steady pace away from the road. The two hunters led us down a trail through a plain. Eventually, we reached a valley on our left side. We stopped to rest and drank some water. The hunters indicated that this was the valley that the others were supposed to blockade while we made our way around the rim of it. We started off again. A steady jog, mile after mile. We saw occasional wildlife that would not come near us. Impala, lion, and wild dogs. All of the wildlife seemed aware of our presence and kept well away. The hunters were taking us along the side of the rim of the valley. Mostly we tracked through plains. But a jungle lurked in the valley, and we could not see far into it. We were wary of a threat of which we were ignorant.

We continued on until dusk, and set up a camp without lighting a fire. We set a watch, and turned in for the night.

*　　*　　*　　*　　*

Cindy was upset that the others were gone, and so was Kirsten. Cindy didn't want to take down her tent at first, but Kirsten made her get to work on it. "Putting up a tent might be a little tricky, but taking it down is easy," she said. Cindy figured it out eventually, and tensions between them eased a little. The camp was coming down slowly as people readied for the coming march and battle. Kirsten decided to head for the main tent as a representative for the trio of girls. She found the tent, but Robbins was busy with the members of his clique.

Robbins was giving orders to a grey-shirted bouncer. "We have plenty of extra guns. Let's recruit some of the men from the town to man the front lines. We don't want them working behind us though; they might shoot some of our own." The man sped away with a translator. After several more conversations like this, Robbins noticed Kirsten and his expression softened. "I know we had to split your group up, but the mission is just too important to jeopardize. I really feel you will be a big help in the blockade. Stay with Danno, and he will help keep you up to speed. We're about ready to move now." Kirsten hadn't gotten a word in, but she nodded and headed back for the others. They agreed that sticking with Danno was a good idea, and they shouldered their packs and found him with a couple of other fans of the band. Danno seemed to be expecting them, and he began a short speech.

"Okay, the people you see here are all buddies. We form a team. We will camp together, eat together, and perform maneuvers together. We will be on the front line of the blockade. Actually, to my knowledge, there is only one line, and we will be a part of it. I will be the team leader, so if I ask you to do something, please do it without question. Please make it clear to someone if you are taking a bathroom break, and don't go far. We will be in the middle of the march, so our duties during the march will be light, but stay alert. When we get to the spot of the blockade, we will cut down a barricade with our machetes. Then, if we have time, we will cut down another barricade behind us to retreat to if necessary. I will give the retreat signal, and hopefully it will be executed as practiced at the firing range. Are there any questions?"

Kirsten raised her hand, "How far are we marching?"

"Only half a day," Danno said. "The rest of the day will be spent making the barricade. Any other questions?" No one seemed to have any other questions. They lined up and walked to where the others were gathering. When everyone had come together, a couple of hunters from the village led the way down a trail. The group strung out along the trail. After an hour or two, they entered the valley, and the forest enveloped them. Many were not in very good shape, and progress was slow. It was dark at times, as the leaves of trees covered the party like a blanket. The march continued.

Eventually, they reached a spot where the valley narrowed. The hunters indicated that this was the ideal spot for a blockade, and Robbins agreed. He spoke to the group.

"This is the spot you're going to get used to," he said. "We are going to hold here when the enemy shows up, and beat them with our superior weaponry. Let's make a barricade here while Danno's team stands lookout. Fan out a little bit and protect us if the enemy comes. All right! Let's get to it."

A hunter came up to Danno and led them a ways up the trail. Then Danno had them spread out to cover as much of the valley as they could, while still having a few people in view of the trail. The girls, Kirsten, Cindy, and April, were along the right hand side. The hunter was with them on the right hand side as well. The other members of their small group spread out along the left hand side of the valley. They had to cover enough terrain that they were basically all alone. Guns were at the ready. They were crouching behind tree trunks. They could hear the construction of the barricade behind them. Machetes chopped at underbrush. Even a few chainsaws were running. It made it hard to discern any sounds in front of them. Would the enemy come creeping through the jungle, making nary a sound? Or would they charge screaming, bearing down on them fast? It played on one's nerves as one waited.

The darkness began to deepen. The racket muted by the forest continued behind them. The guns grew heavy. Kirsten had her gun pointed in the air when someone tapped her on the shoulder. She had had no idea that someone was behind her, and she turned, startled. It was the hunter. He put his finger to his lips and motioned back to the barricade. He collected the rest of the group on the right hand side, and they filed back to the spot they would try to hold. Meeting up with them was the group on the left hand side. Danno spoke to them quietly.

"The barricade is almost finished," he said. "We are to withdraw behind it now." They filed back down the path, and it was evident that good work had been done on the barricade. It stretched across the valley floor at chest height. It was made mostly of small trees with the limbs still attached, but big trunks also impeded progress. There was a gap through the barricade where the path was, but after Danno's group came through, it was quickly sealed with logs and brush. Robbins and a cadre of grey shirted muscular men met them behind the barricade.

"Good look-out," Robbins said. "I guess there was no sign of the enemy?"

"Nothing that we saw." said Danno. "You were making enough of a racket that they might have stayed away."

"I doubt it," Robbins replied. "We were at our most vulnerable while working on the barricade, and they would have profited by an attack. Good work, anyway. Let's set up camp." There was plenty of space where the brush had been cleared to set up tents, and camp fires were lit. This time, Cindy set up her own tent almost without any help, and she looked proud of herself. Danno's team was not included in any part of the watch overnight, so after a dinner of army rations, they turned in for bed and slept through the night.

*   *   *   *   *

Wolf lay in front of the door of my tent. He had been sleeping all night, but his presence there soothed me, and I had no dreams. In the morning, we did the normal morning camping things, and Devon announced something to our small group.

"I got a call on the radio," he said. "The blockade is set up! The enemy has not yet attacked, and they are preparing to set up the retreat blockade." There were some cheers from the group, and Jericho stood up.

"We better get moving," he said. "They are counting on us to destroy the leadership of this menace." Everyone took down their tents and shouldered their packs. Ten was our number, and we had our guns at the ready. The hunters led us along the rim of the valley again, and the tense journey continued. Wolf ran down a small mammal for breakfast and crunched it happily. He was really in his element out here in the wild. We continued along the trail, and looked to our left, down into the darkness of the trees. Although the early morning had been raucous with bird noises, now it was strangely silent. A lion paced our journey, staying a constant distance behind us. After awhile, he lay down and let us retreat into the distance. We continued, until a hunter motioned at Jericho. Jericho raised his hand, and we crouched silently. The hunter walked to the rim of the valley, and looked carefully over the rim of it into the darkness. He came back and talked to Jericho.

"I cannot see anything, but I believe a large group is passing by below us. I can tell from the way the wildlife is reacting, and I believe I can just hear them."

Jericho thought for a moment. "It may be that the leadership of this army is bringing up the rear. Or perhaps they are not traveling with the army at all. This is what our previous intelligence tells us. After the army passes, we should cut down into the valley and travel back along the trail to their original camp. If their leader is not there, we will double-time it back to attack the rear of the army."

The hunter spoke. "There is a way down into the valley not too much farther ahead. It is steep, but passable."

Jericho decided for the group. "After the army passes, that is the route we will take, then. Devon, radio the others that the army is on the move." Devon did so, and we made our way along the rim of the valley until we found the trail down into it. After the hunter judged that the army had passed by, we waited about fifteen minutes and started to make our way into the valley. It was very steep, and it was awkward carrying our guns and packs while trying to hold onto trees on the way down. When we reached the valley floor, we indeed saw the indications that a large group of people had passed by. They had tramped a wide path through the forest.

Jericho spoke up again. "We will leave our packs here now, hidden off the trail. We will carry guns, water, and trail bars only. We will go quietly, but quickly. We will try to surprise the enemy's leader, and any forces he has left." We did as he asked, and hid our packs just off the trail. Then we took off toward the source of the tracks that passed us. It certainly was easy going, as they had tramped and broken a path for us. We followed their trail for hours, until it seemed that it might be time to stop for lunch. We ate a few trail bars, and listened carefully for any stragglers. After less than a twenty minute break, we continued along the trail. The trail was straight as an arrow along the valley floor.

The hunter spoke. "These people were moving quickly," he said.

Jericho responded. "Then we should move quickly too. Pick up the pace a little." We had been moving at a jog already, but now we ran. The hunter took the lead, easily leaping over roots and rocks. The rest of us matched his pace as best we could, but Devon was burdened by the radio and brought up the rear. The hunter stopped short, and all of us could see a clearing up ahead. There was a fire smoldering in the middle of it, and a group of African men were standing around the fire. Behind them a massive, doughy, albino shape stood. He was the man from my dreams, with a blue crystal embedded in his forehead.

"They are here!" He yelled, in a deep gravelly voice. "Destroy them!" The African men turned with a roar and ran towards us. We lined up and went to one knee as quickly as we could, and we prepared to fire into the clearing.

*   *   *   *   *

Back at the blockade, people were just stirring in the early morning, but Robbins was walking among the tents. "Up, everyone! Get breakfast and get moving. We must construct a retreat barricade today." People got out of their tents and stretched, perhaps with a feeling that danger was not as close now that they had had a good nights sleep.

Danno rounded up his group and gave them the news. "We are to be on watch again today. I guess we did such a good job that we have the job again. This time we will stand behind the main barricade, so we will be that much safer. Let's spread out." Kirsten and Cindy were along the right hand side within sight of each other. Again, the chopping and sawing began behind them. Kirsten was straining to watch the forest ahead of her. She did not know whether the enemy would come sneaking up from a devious route, or whether they would come running straight at her. It was easier this time to hold her gun. She could rest it on the barricade. The time passed. The noise of the construction was a constant disturbance to her. She couldn't seem to get used to it. The time passed again, more slowly. Then she felt a presence behind her, and glanced back. Robbins was coming her way, flanked with gunmen.

"We are reinforcing the barricade," he said. "We just got word that the enemy army is on the move towards us. It is a large group, and they are coming quickly." Robbins moved on down the line, assigning men to the front barricade. To Kirsten, it felt like danger had multiplied sevenfold. Before, the menace had been a possibility, something she had believed in her mind, but not with her heart. Now, every fiber of her being felt the impending battle. The noise of construction slowed, but she could see a retreat barricade taking shape behind her. As the reinforcements spread out along the front barricade, Danno's group clustered together.

Cindy seemed almost panicked. "I heard it was a large group," she said. "Do you think it will overwhelm us?"

Danno tried to allay her fears. "We are the ones who are prepared," he said. "We have superior weaponry, and a task force that will destroy their leader. Once the crystal is broken, the battle will be won." Cindy still seemed nervous, but the group turned their attention once again outward. Lunch was brought, and the work on the retreat barricade was finished. A group of about 50 manned the first barricade, including a large group of villagers who had not trained with the weapons. They were spread out between the Americans, who were standing by to help them if they had problems. They hadn't waited long, when a faint screaming was heard in the distance. Everyone tensed, and then they saw the army of Africans painted black running down the trail. They came five wide at the center, and seemed heedless to the bushes they trampled. They were horribly scarred and looked bent on destruction.

*　　*　　*　　*　　*

At the clearing, the albino leader exhorted his troops. There were ten of them, horribly scarred, and they didn't have any weapons. I fired into the throng, and one of them fell backwards, hit in the chest. The rest of our group fired as well, and the men spun and twisted about, battered by the bullets. I looked behind me briefly to see if it had been some kind of trap, but no one seemed to be coming from behind us. The game was over before it had even started. But then the Africans stood up again. Their wounds were hideous, and yet they charged again. We fired again, knocking them every which way, but they closed.

Jericho yelled out. "They won't die! They are some kind of zombie! Shoot for the knees!" I tried to readjust my aim, but hitting the knee of a moving target is tough, and I didn't know if I succeeded. A couple did go down and seemed to have trouble getting up. But suddenly, they were among us. Jericho shouted again. "Devon, call Robbins! He must know of this development!" Devon broke off and started to use the radio, but I was too busy to watch him make the call. I dropped my gun and used my staff to keep one away from me. Some of our group were firing point blank into the zombies, but confusion reigned. Davies, the bouncer, grappled with one hand to hand. He was punishing it, pulping its body, but it seemed to feel no pain. Jericho was clubbing one with his gun. He got behind it and broke its neck, but it continued fighting. Its head leaned at a strange angle. Wolf was the one that kept the battle from becoming a rout. He was everywhere, knocking them down, ripping their throats out. After a time, the battle became eerily quiet, as the zombies quit their yelling and shrieking. I kept hitting the zombie that was attacking me in the chest with the end of my staff, keeping him away. Jericho had pulled out a knife and sliced the head off of his zombie and pushed the decapitated face into the dirt. The body was stumbling around, trying to find someone to engage. Then Jericho jumped on the back of my zombie and slit its throat. He sawed at the neck and pulled the head off by brute force with his left hand. I glanced at the other battles, and saw Davies go down. The zombie broke his neck, and Davies lay on the grass face down.

Jericho finished decapitating the zombie that had been attacking me and got my attention. "Get Wolf and go attack the leader. We'll keep these zombies busy while you two take care of him. Please hurry, this is not going well." I ran after Wolf just as he tore the throat out of another zombie. I got his attention and urged him to follow me after the leader. As we looked into the clearing, we saw that the leader was nowhere to be found. He had run away! I looked back at the battle, and I saw Davies getting up from the ground. His neck had been broken, but now he was standing. His head lay at a strange angle, but he let out a tortured yell. Then he started attacking one of the other members of our group. The man seemed surprised that

Davies was attacking, and took a number of blows before he was able to react. I turned my attention back to Wolf.

Wolf was sniffing all around the clearing. "The stench of a dead thing has gone this way." He said. I followed him as he led the way deeper into the jungle. I had my staff ready as we quickly followed the trail. We went on for a time weaving between trees, when suddenly, the pale leader of the zombies crashed in from the side. He had circled back on the trail and surprised us! He fell on Wolf and tackled him, and Wolf yelped in pain. They rolled around as the doughy golem tightened his grip. Wolf could not bend his neck enough to bite him. I hit the albino golem with my staff, but it seemed to have little effect. Then I jumped on his back and tried to choke him with it.

*   *   *   *   *

Back at the barricade, gunfire erupted from the center of the line. Danno's group was firing from the right, and the evil African army was flung back. The front went down, and the Africans behind them tripped over the recently fallen. The firing continued, and slowly the barricade force realized what the strike force had realized. The evil army of Africans seemed indestructible. The ones that were shot up terribly still got up and limped toward the barricade. Just at that point, the radio squawked, and information about the zombies came in from the strike force. Robbins yelled at the radio man, "Yes! We are realizing that now! Do you have any useful information for us?" The radio went dead. Robbins walked up and down the line. "At all costs, we must keep them on the other side of the barricade!" He said. "Use the machetes and chainsaws when they reach the barricade!" Some people were dispatched to the retreat barricade to get the tools that had been left lying around.

The withering fire from all sides crushed the zombies advance, but there were many of them coming, and they managed to make headway against the firepower. Soon, they were mashed up against the barricade, trying to climb it. Machetes were brought into play, chopping off hands and arms, even heads. The concentration of zombies was at the center of the trail, but they began to spread out along the edges. They clawed at the barricade, beginning to destroy its integrity. Kirsten fired again and again into the throng, but to no effect. Suddenly, at one point, the zombies came over the barricade near Danno's group. A few of them were among the defenders, and guns could no longer be used. A grey-shirted bouncer leapt into the fray with a chainsaw, and he punished them. But confusion reigned for the moment, and several defenders went down. Robbins brought a couple of reinforcements to keep more zombies from pouring into the gap, and the rupture was healed.

The battle became fiercer as more zombies strung out along the line. Kirsten noticed that Cindy was down on the ground, and went to help her up. Cindy looked pale, and let out a horrible cry. She shook off Kirsten's help and launched herself at the red-haired girl. Kirsten was taken by surprise, and fended off the attack by holding her rifle sideways. "What the hell?" She said. "Cindy! Stop it!" Cindy's eyes were rolled back into her head, and she made no reply. Robbins saw what was going on, and he slugged Cindy across the face with his fist. Her head snapped back, but she continued to fight. Robbins saw a bad gash across her throat that had bled out all over her clothes. However, it did not bleed now.

"She's dead!" He cried. "That's the secret. If you are killed by one of these zombies, you turn into one." Cindy turned on him and tried to choke him, but he shot her in the leg. She stumbled, but continued to attack. "That's it, that's all the proof I need." He said, and called for someone with a machete. The man with the machete quickly dismembered her and decapitated her. Kirsten cried out as if she was the one being cut, but Robbins took a moment to comfort her. "We can't have an enemy behind the lines. It would just cause chaos."

Kirsten replied. "What if they all return to normal when the crystal is broken? She may have had a chance." Robbins shook his head.

"These people are all dead," he said. "They will just die when the crystal is broken." He looked toward another part of the line where people were in trouble. "I have to go now. Keep up your spirits." He departed with a few of his entourage in tow.

Kirsten looked at the dismembered body of her rival. Still it moved, clawing at the earth and flexing disgustingly. She shuddered, and thought back to the times that Cindy had annoyed her. However, Cindy was her only link to the small group that had traveled all this way. She turned her attention back to the barricade.

* * * * *

Wolf and I struggled with the pale golem. I was on his back, choking him with the staff, but he didn't seem to need the air. Wolf was imprisoned in his arms, and could

164

not bite effectively. I pulled the staff away from the golem's throat and smashed it down on the back of his head. The golem roared and released one of his arms to strike at me. It was like a sledgehammer, and it tossed me aside like a leaf in the wind. I dropped the staff, and it fell to the earth away from me. The golem let out a cry of triumph, and he leapt for the staff. At the last moment, I kicked it away from him, and it slid deeper into the woods. The golem went after it, but now Wolf was on his feet. He quickly positioned himself between the staff and the golem. The golem crouched, and spread his hands. At that moment, Wolf sprang heroically. The golem may have outweighed Wolf slightly, but it seemed that Wolf was faster, for he slipped in between the outstretched arms of the golem. Wolf locked his jaws on the golem's throat but could not rip it out. The golem gave Wolf a bear hug that looked vicious, but Wolf was not letting go. I scrambled for the staff, giving the combat a wide berth. Soon, it was in my hands, and I turned back to the battle. Wolf had pushed the golem over and lay on top of him, but the golem's massive arms still clamped around his midsection. I hurried to the battle, but it seemed to be a deadlock, and I didn't know what to do. The golem thrashed around, kicking up leaves like a trapped animal, and his head fetched up against a tree. I saw my chance and took it. While Wolf held his head pinned against the tree, I touched an end of the staff to the blue jewel in the golem's forehead. Then I concentrated on the spirit of the forest, and all the life it encompassed. The golem tried to shake his head from side to side, but I kept it pinned down with the staff. I thought of the majestic Redwoods on the west coast, and the strange thick-trunked

165

Baobab trees here in Africa.

Suddenly, the evil blue crystal exploded, taking much of the golem's head with it. Wolf was hit by flying shards, but he could not back away, because the golem's arms still held him. The pieces of the blue crystal melted, and with that, the body of the golem turned into a pale slurry that spread out onto the forest floor. It created a pool of slime that Wolf stepped out of. He was dirty with pale muck. He limped around for a moment, and then fell on his side. Wolf coughed, and blood sprayed out of his mouth. He managed to stand again, and I leaned over by him.

"Are you alright?" I asked. His head lifted, and he tried to walk a little.

"I can continue," he said softly. "Let us go slowly though." I agreed with him thoroughly, and we started slowly back down the trail. I thought about how rashly we had come down the trail, ripe for ambush. It had almost ended in disaster, but in the end, the battle had been won. We walked slowly down the trail making it back to the enemy's clearing. In front of us was an astonishing sight. Jericho and the other members of the strike team were still battling zombies. It was mostly over, it was true, but two zombies still fought against the others. Jericho saw us and yelled.

"No, No! Don't come back here until you have killed their leader. We can handle this now."

I ran up, and looked around in confusion. "We destroyed the leader. I broke the crystal in his head, and he melted into a pool of slime."

Jericho looked stricken. "This is horrible!" He said.

166

"The zombies are still fighting." As he spoke, they were dismembered by the rest of the team. "Davies and Devon both turned on us. We had to kill them." The pieces of zombie were still quivering on the ground. Jericho quickly picked up the radio. It seemed undamaged. He called up the team back at the barricade.

"We've killed the leader, but it appears that the zombies continue to fight." He shouted into the headset. The man on the other end of the radio sounded shocked, but told them to get back to the village as soon as possible. Jericho handed the radio to one of the others and spoke to the small company. "We have to double time it back to the village. I know you're tired, but our only way back home is the buses. The other team is going to try to hold the zombies back until we get there."

We immediately grabbed our guns and water. We started trotting back to the place we had entered the valley. As soon as we reached that, we climbed up the steep slope. The hunter led us along the rim of the valley back toward the village, but we knew we had an all day and all night march ahead of us.

* * * * *

Kirsten was back at the barricade. The fighting was fierce, and it seemed that the supply of zombies was inexhaustible. She fired blindly over the barricade into the oncoming horde, but she seemed to do little damage. Robbins made his way behind the barricade, calling to the small force. "We must hold here all night, till dawn if necessary. That will give the others time to get back."

Kirsten wondered. "Time to get back?" She thought to herself. "They should stay until they've destroyed the

167

leader. Something's gone wrong. I hope they're all okay." A zombie clawed its way over the barricade, and she shot it in the face. It fell back, blinded.

Danno stepped next to her. "Good job!" He said. "I've heard that they destroyed the leader, but that the zombies do not die. Don't tell the others or they may get disheartened." Kirsten thought that might be a good idea if she ever wanted to see the others again. She reloaded her rifle and continued to shoot over the barricade. Their tremendous firepower was the only thing that was saving them from being overwhelmed. Here and there a zombie would make it over the barricade, but then the chainsaws would come into play, and it would be dismembered quickly.

Night began to fall, and the zombies continued to attack relentlessly. In the darkness, more of them climbed closer to the top of the barricade before being pushed back. It was harder to target the zombies as they came at the defenders. The zombies showed no signs of tiring. Now Kirsten was firing directly as the evil creatures came over the top of the barricade. The fight went on and on into the night.

Over on the other wing of the barricade, a group of zombies broke through the defenses. At least half a dozen made it over the top, and they started to sow chaos in the ranks. The chainsaws and machetes came into play, as the fighting was too close for guns. Then one of the chainsaws ran out of gas! The zombie that was closest roared, and overwhelmed the poor man who had been wielding the chainsaw. Soon the man had fallen to the zombies. Robbins brought his cadre into the fight, and the zombies were dismembered, but several men of the defender's group had to be destroyed as well. It was a grim business. It went on like this long into the night. The defenders became tired and the zombies continued to fight.

*　　*　　*　　*　　*

On the trail, it was a race to get to the village. I had never been so tired, both from sleep deprival and running. We had been alternating running and walking for hours, and were carrying only guns and water. The hunters seemed to be having little trouble, but the rest of us were hard put to keep up the pace they were setting. Even Wolf, wounded as he was, was having trouble keeping up the pace. Every once in a while he had to stop and choke up spittle and traces of blood. The trek continued. Jericho called a halt to the running so that we could continue at a walk. There were eight of us and Wolf.

I increased my pace slightly until I was even with Jericho. "What are we going to do when we get back to the village?" I asked. "The zombies fight on even though I have destroyed the crystal."

Jericho nodded wearily. "Robbins will have to decide," he said. "I expect we will take some of the village children back with us to America. I believe Africa is in real trouble." We walked on down the trail. Once we had caught our breath, we began to run again. Luckily, the moon lit our way down the trail. The wildlife seemed more threatening at night, as if they weren't afraid any more. The distance that usually separated them from us became smaller, and they seemed more eager to defend their territory. There were no actual incidents though. Intellectually we knew that we must make all speed back to the village, because the others were defending a hopeless battle. But the reality was the wish to slow the pace just a little to ease our tired muscles. The reality was the wish to ask for a halt to recover our breath. Jericho exhorted us to Herculean efforts on the trail, and we followed his lead. The running and walking continued unabated.

*　　*　　*　　*　　*

The zombies at the barricade were starting to overwhelm the forces of The Dugouts. Robbins called the retreat, and they went into a prearranged drill. A couple of people doused the barricade with gasoline, and they lit it as the others retreated behind the retreat barricade. The maneuver was a mixed success. The barricade did not light immediately, as the wood was green. Zombies came over the top while people were still trying to get through the openings in the retreat barricade. Some of the people were firing behind them at the zombies that were coming for them. Soon, the barricade was burning in earnest, but a few zombies were already attacking the retreat barricade. Some of the defenders had been pulled down and killed in the confusion. They added to the ranks of the zombies. Robbins told the man with the radio to call the vanguard group.

"We have taken some losses here and have been forced to retreat to the second barricade. This is the last stand. Where are you?" He relayed to the radio man. The call went through, and the reply was that the group should be at the village by dawn. It was about three hours until dawn, so Robbins decided to rally the troops. "Only one or two more hours!" He shouted along the line. "Then we fire this barricade and retreat to the village. The fighters

170

let out a halfhearted cheer as they continued to fire over the barricade. April and Kirsten were fighting together. They fired over the barricade in tandem, and covered each other when one had to reload. There was still a tremendous amount of ammunition left.

Danno stayed near to them, as leader of his team. He shouted encouragement to the others. "Only a little while longer now! Then we hightail it back to town." The flames from the first barricade had been put out by the mass of zombies struggling to get over it. They seemed to feel no pain. Already they were making concerted attacks at the second barricade. The battle went on, but the defenders held till the appointed hour. This time, they burned the barricade before any zombies could even get over, and then the retreat began in earnest.

*　*　*　*　*

I ran down the trail, and familiar signs from the village began to appear. Dawn was breaking over the hills, and it seemed to wash away the cares of our bleak enterprise. We had made it! The buses were right where we had left them, and we started the motors while we waited for the others. Soon enough, they began to arrive. They showed up in small groups, looking anxiously back over their shoulders. I could understand their concern. Wolf and I were standing in front of the lead bus when we spotted Kirsten and April. Kirsten shouted with joy and ran up for a big hug. Then she hugged Wolf as well, and he said, "Careful, please." April was looking around for Devon, and then her eyes rested on mine. I just shook my head solemnly. She looked away as if she didn't know what to do. Kirsten turned to me quickly. "Cindy was killed too. I'm so sorry." I was just numb. I didn't feel anything at that moment but a passing wish that we had had a chance to be closer.

At that moment, Robbins came trotting up. "They're not far behind us!" He shouted. "Everybody into the buses." That began a scramble to get onto the buses as quickly as possible. As soon as we were loaded and ready to move, the scarred and burned zombies came out of the forest. We began to drive away, and the zombies pounded at the sides of the buses and wailed. Some of the windows were broken as the zombies reached for us. The drivers just drove away however, and the zombies were unable to keep up. We made for the village.

When we reached the outskirts, the villagers surrounded us. They were cheering and waving their hands. After we halted, the villagers saw the look on our faces. Some of the villagers that had been with us through the fight exited the buses and began explaining things to the people around us. The cheering quieted, and then ceased completely. The grey-haired village elder pushed his way through the crowd and asked us what had happened. Robbins met him and explained that we had killed the leader, but that the enemy were zombies and could not be killed. He explained that they were now on the way to the village.

"We can take a few of you back to America with us." He said. "We will save some of your children." There was much confusion at this, and the mothers started grabbing their kids and pushing them forward. They ran back to their dwellings and brought clothes and toys, mostly drums. Some of the drums seemed to be prized heirlooms they wished to leave with their children. Then one of the men who had been with us for the fight leveled his gun at Robbins.

"I will go too," he said. Robbins stared at him evenly, but did not speak. At that moment several of the other villagers tackled him and took him to the ground.

The grey-haired man spoke. "Forgive his cowardice," he said. "We know you have done everything in your power to save us."

Robbins replied. "We will leave any extra guns and ammunition we have with you. It will do little good against these creatures, but maybe it will give you a chance to escape." Soon the buses were filled to their capacity and more. It was clear that it would be an uncomfortable ride back to Nairobi. The buses started to move with children crying and parents running after the buses waving and crying as well. The village was left in the past, and a place will never be the same once you leave it behind.

I sat in the back of the bus with Kirsten, April, and Wolf. Wolf took up a whole seat to himself. He lay there panting, trying to gather his strength. We drove for a long while, ready to make the city of Eldoret. On the outskirts of Eldoret, we came upon a gas station. The buses pulled in, but the place was deserted. Overturned merchandise littered the floor. A small group gathered around Robbins as he made the decision.

"We need the gas," he said. "Let's pump it and be on our way." Luckily the pumps were working, and soon the tanks were topped off, along with any gas containers we had. We loaded up again and headed in to Eldoret proper. When we reached the city, we found chaos. Fires were raging, and zombies walked the streets. We quickly armed ourselves, and pointed the guns out the windows. There were accidents everywhere and many of the streets were blocked. Local people tried to board the buses as zombies pulled them apart.

Robbins went to the driver in the lead bus who was one of our African guides. "Get us out of here!" He shouted. "Make for the country the easiest, shortest way." Fortunately, most of the usable cars had already left Eldoret, and there wasn't much traffic. We ran down a few zombies, and a few people as well, but we made it out of the city. Soon we were on a road that would take us in a circuitous route to Nairobi.

We traveled on and on. We traveled through the night, as the drivers switched off. Owners of gas stations were clearly nervous, and some were out of gas. Some of the towns were infested with zombies, but others were clear of the invasion. However, it was clear that Africa would fall soon to a plague like no other. We drove for a long time, and Nairobi was then on the horizon. It didn't seem that the zombie hordes had yet come to Nairobi, but it was clear that everyone was nervous. We drove straight for the airport. When we reached it, the way to the tarmac was blocked by guards. An official from the airport remembered us and shouted up to the buses.

"All planes have been taken over by the country of Kenya!" He said. "Your plane is now the property of Kenya!" I don't think he realized what kind of firepower we had. We all thrust our guns out the windows and pointed them at the guards. One of the guards got on a radio for support, but we drove through them heedlessly. Luckily there was no shooting, and soon we were making our way to where our plane had been left. The plane and pilot were there, and the pilot looked quite relieved to see us. We loaded the plane as fast as possible as Kenyan guards began collecting near us. We kept them covered carefully until we finished boarding the plane. Then we taxied to the runway and flew into the sky. Africa seemed lost, but we were on our way back to America!

❖ Chapter 11

"I think the slain care little if they sleep or rise again; and we, the living, wherefore should we ache with counting all our lost ones?"
Aeschylus, Agamemnon

Conversation was heated on the plane back to America. Topics included things like: What would happen to the people of Africa now that there was this horrible scourge, would Africa be quarantined by a military force, the United States must know of the depth of this disaster, and what steps were they taking. The talk went on and on, until people began to drop off to sleep. We continued to fly back to America.

Wolf was not sleeping, and I asked him how he was doing.

"I am getting better," he said in his terse way. I wanted to stay up a little longer, but eventually, I slept with the others.

The flight was long, and it is uncomfortable sleeping in a plane. I woke several times during the flight. Then, the captain spoke over the intercom. "We are reaching our final approach to JFK international. Soon we will be home again. Robbins would like to say a few things."

Then Robbins's voice came on the intercom. "I would like to take this moment to remember those of us who did not make it back. We started this mission with a large heart, and we did everything we could for those villagers in Africa. We succeeded in destroying the leader, but unfortunately, it was not enough. I want to thank every one of you who took a chance by coming with us to

176

Africa, especially those of you who lost someone on this trip. You'll all be home soon. Thank you again." The intercom fell silent.

April looked at us uncertainly. "I don't have a home to go to, really. And when I lost Devon, I lost any reason to have a home."

Kirsten replied. "You stay with us. I'm sure we are going to travel somewhere exciting, and it will keep your mind off things." April laid her head on Kirsten's shoulder and closed her eyes. Kirsten put her arm around April's head and tried to comfort her. I was in agreement with Kirsten. I thought having Wolf around would be good for April too. It's always good to have animals around in times of sorrow.

The captain came on the intercom again. "There seems to be something wrong with the radio on our plane, or at the tower at JFK," he said. "I'm not getting any response from the tower. But we have to land anyway. We're low on fuel. Please buckle up and get ready for landing. We have to land the old-fashioned way." Everyone (except Wolf) put on their seatbelts. The children from Africa had been drumming spontaneously during the trip, but now the drums were stowed away safely in the compartments above. The plane descended, and landed safely on the tarmac. It was an eerie view out the windows of the plane. There didn't seem to be any other planes in the airport. The place was deserted. Everyone was looking out of the windows as the plane taxied to the charter gate.

The plane made it to the gate, and Robbins came on the intercom. "Everyone stay on the plane until we figure out what's going on." A few of the grey shirted security guys deplaned with Robbins and Jericho. They were all heavily armed, and they walked toward the airport. They had just about made it all the way, when a group of horribly scarred men burst out of the doorway. Their heads lolled on their sides, and they ran forward. Immediately, Robbins' men opened fire, and knocked them down, but the deathless group continued their fight. Eventually, all of them had to be taken down with machetes. The party from the plane was victorious, but what had happened to the people of New York? A man was running at the plane from the other side of the tarmac, and the grey shirted men swiveled to cover him. He raised his hands and approached more slowly. He was an airport employee, and he didn't appear to be a zombie. He had some conversation with Robbins' group, and then Robbins came back onto the plane.

"We need a group to go get fuel," he said. "We must fly out of here now. New York has mostly fallen to the zombies. Nowhere in the world is safe! Who wants to get the fuel?" There were cries of disbelief and horror as he said this, but a few raised their hands, Danno included. A small group left the plane and went with the airport employee to get fuel. Robbins' group stayed to guard the plane. Soon enough, Danno was back with a fuel truck. They started fueling the plane quickly. Zombies came out of the airport sporadically, but there didn't seem to be a concerted effort to get us. As time went by, there were more and more of them, and the battle became heated. There were no barricades to protect the fighters, and several fell to the zombies. Danno's group finished fueling the plane, and everyone got back on. People were firing to keep the zombies off of the stairway, and we pulled it up in time. The employee from the airport was with us as well, and the plane taxied back onto the runway. The zombies chased us, and tried to cling to the plane as it took off, but we were away safely.

Now the conversation started again, and it was no longer Africa that we were talking about, but the Earth itself. No one knew where a safe place to go would be if America was infected.

Robbins came on the speaker again. "We've decided to go to Lincoln, Nebraska," he said. "We have a warehouse there, and we've been able to call some of our friends there that say the zombie influence has not yet reached there. You are all welcome to stay with us at the warehouse until we figure out what to do." The flight continued. One of the grey-shirted men came back to me and asked me to come up to the front of the plane. There was a private meeting room where Robbins, Jericho, and a few others were talking.

Robbins looked up as I came in, and asked me a question. "In your travels, did you ever discover where the seat of power of the Borzhat was? We are discussing taking the fight to them now. That may be the only way to save the Earth." I thought back and remembered my dream of the zombie leader.

"I had a dream before the battle in Africa," I said.

"The leader of the zombies told me of a temple called Kreaco-Ath deep within a mountain of fire. There are three high priests of the Borzhat there that use the Primus crystal. Perhaps if we destroy that crystal, Earth may be saved."

Robbins looked at me with a strange expression. It was almost as if he knew something and was surprised, or as if he felt a bond with me that he didn't want to share.

"I know that place," he said. "It lies on a world that we were on not too long ago."

One of the grey-shirted men spoke. "They are too powerful on that world," he said. "Their minions overrun everything we do there."

Jericho responded. "We could take them by surprise. If we showed up near the mountain, maybe we could sneak in before the forces of the world are mobilized against us."

Robbins made the decision. "I think if the energy is right we could appear near the mountain. But we must find care for these children first. Then we will take any who will come on another mission. We have much to plan for." Then he looked at me. "Thank you very much for your information." It seemed clear that I was dismissed. I went back to my seat.

Kirsten perked up when I sat down. "What did they want?" She asked.

I spoke quietly to our small group. "We have a mission to your world, Kirsten." I said. "We are going to take the fight into the mountains that you described." Once again I felt a sense of overwhelming responsibility. It seemed that I, like Atlas, bore the Earth itself on my shoulders. "There is a first crystal called the Primus Crystal. Perhaps if we destroy that crystal, all the evil works of the Borzhat will perish."

Wolf quietly spoke. "It is enough that we fight continually. To make a difference, all we can do is try."

The flight continued on for a long time, but eventually we started to make our approach to the airport. We landed safely, and we taxied to a gate. White vans came out to meet us, and we soon were loaded in them and heading to a warehouse that was not really very close to Lincoln. We made quite a convoy of white vans, as all the children were with us as well. We still had all our weapons. They did not split up our group that had been working so well. Kirsten, April, Danno, Wolf and I were all in the same van. Soon everyone was at the warehouse, and we unpacked and entered. Everyone needed a shower, and fortunately there were some bathrooms and facilities there. There was a stage in the warehouse, and instruments were already waiting for the band. The kids were overjoyed to be in an open space, and they ran around laughing and shrieking.

Robbins got onstage and spoke into one of the microphones. "We are having a concert tomorrow night at midnight," he said. "It is an open air concert at a farm not too far from here. I know many of you have nowhere else to go, so we hope that you will come with us. We are planning on taking you into battle again, this time on another world. Anyone who wishes may stay here at the warehouse, but remember… the earth may be doomed!"

Robbins left the stage, and people started talking seriously with each other. It was almost unanimous to go to the concert and follow The Dugouts wherever they went. It was getting towards evening again, and there were plenty of sleeping mats at the warehouse. People began spreading out their mats on the floor next to people that they knew. Only a few lights were on so people could find the bathrooms. The children from Africa were holding up remarkably well. They weren't crying much, even if they did miss their parents. I dropped off to sleep.

*   *   *   *   *

The next day was spent scrounging up supplies. The meals and ammunition were almost gone, so people were sent to get those items. We absolutely cleaned out gun stores of their ammunition, and we still didn't have as much as we had going into Africa. That ammunition had been ordered factory direct. Food was a little easier, but it wasn't going to be prepackaged meals. A lot of peanut butter was purchased, along with pasta with powdered flavoring. I'm sure we cleaned the stores out of cheese in a can too. We visited local laundromats and did a lot of packing and repacking. A group of grey-shirted men from the band tried to find foster homes for the children, but without much success. There was a lot of paperwork involved, and none of the children had papers. It was pretty clear it would be a long process. Robbins made the decision to take the children with us. He felt that Earth was such a dangerous place that no danger we could take them into would be worse.

In the late afternoon, we loaded up the vans and went to the farm. There was much to do to prepare for the concert. Parking had to be arranged. The stage and lights had to be set up. Dinner had to be prepared for a hundred people. People were talking and wondering about what would happen and where they were going. Evening began to fall. Along with the darkness, people who knew about the concert from Lincoln and neighboring towns began to show up. The moon was full, and it hung high in the clear night sky. As everyone began to get more excited for the show and the impending trip, there was a tremendous flash in the sky. We all looked up, and saw an incredible sight. The moon had a corona! There was a fiery red light all around the edges of the moon. The corona was at least as bright as the moon itself, but an orange-red color, like the sun. No one could imagine what it could mean. People looked at the sky in wonder.

"It is a good omen for our journey!" said one of the African translators. There were other theories.

"It's some kind of St. Elmo's Fire," said a young man. The time for the concert was still hours away.

Kirsten came up to me. "Do you think the moon is getting bigger?" She said. I looked at it carefully. It was clearly much bigger than it had been, at least half again as big as it usually was. The corona was also still in evidence.

"It is bigger," I said. "That must mean it's getting closer." The instruments were set up, but The Dugouts were not to take the stage earlier than midnight. It was only nine o'clock. As time went on, the moon became bigger and bigger. At first it was the size of a quarter. Then it became the size of your fist. Soon it was the size of a dinner plate. The seas and craters were easily visible to the naked eye. The people at the concert became frantic. At 11 o'clock, the moon was the size of a carousel. Part of it was in eclipse from the earth's shadow. Still, the band refused to come on. It became obvious that the moon was going to strike the earth with catastrophic consequences. Finally, at midnight, the band took the stage. We were able to see them in the moon's eerie augmented glow. No lights were needed at all, and the lights didn't come on. The guitarist started playing a monotonous riff low on the fretboard. The drummer played along with him on the cymbals, while Robbins and Danno stayed out of it. After many bars of this, Danno mimicked the guitarists tune on his bass. Robbins stepped up to the mic.

"The earth is lost!" He shouted. "The moon will crash into the earth and destroy the evil that has come to overwhelm us. It is the ultimate answer, sent from powers beyond our control. Now we must take as many of you with us as we can to a place where the evil originates. We will enter their temple and destroy the Primus Crystal in an effort to restore balance to the universe. During this song, you must stay as still as possible in order to be taken with us."

Then Robbins stepped away from the microphone and started dancing. The music became very fast, and people could hardly help but move in time to it. Robbins sang of a tree that sprouted other trees where its branches hit the ground. It was a tremendous growth that all originated from one source. The music slowed from its frantic pace. The tempo became slower and slower, and people were more able to stay still. The glow from the moon made a strange white daylight on the farm, and it was unusual seeing everyone staying still to the music.

Then Robbins yelled. "A big thank you to Changeo! studios!" With that, things began to change.

My feet became literally rooted to the ground. Bark ran up my legs. My arms raised into the air and became branches. Bark closed around my face. The last things I saw were similar changes to the other people in the audience. Everyone was turning into trees! The Dugouts continued to play slower and slower, and my thoughts

184

also became slower. It seemed that only the music was important now, and it guided us. At first we had been budding out in spring, but then leaves of summer quickly appeared. Now we were already in fall, and the leaves were falling. A wind swirled through the new forest that we had become, and leaves fell rapidly from the trees. It was as if our consciousness was falling with the leaves. The leaves were swept up into the sky. They seemed to travel through time and space with music entwining them. The leaves then fell on a rocky slope, and the music became louder. The pile of leaves became a pile of people on the ground, and the music reached its climax. There was a clash of cymbals, and the song ended. We had once again journeyed to another place.

The group of fans stood up slowly, and, as if in answer to the band's song, the African children began drumming. The earth was about to be destroyed, if it had not already been, and we were on our way to fight the people responsible.

Our group got up off the ground. Somehow, The Dugout's stage had been transported with them, so they still had their musical instruments. Our journey to this world had been strange and relaxing. I had never meditated before, but it seemed that I had had a long relaxing time meditating. I felt as if I understood the thought process of a tree as I never had before. We had landed on the bottom slopes of a mountain.

Robbins spoke out to the crowd. "We will head into the mountain to search out the three priests of the Borzhat and destroy them. Get with your team leaders and form your groups so we can organize. We must move quickly while we have the element of surprise." The groups were formed. Jericho and some of the grey-shirted security would take the lead, while our group would be in the middle. Robbins would take the rear with the African children. Our group gathered around Danno. Kirsten was happy to be back on her own world, even if it was at a place she had never been before.

She spoke. "I guess you will have to stay here since your world has been destroyed. I don't think anything we do will change that. Our world has many problems. It is almost completely regimented. There is only a small creative segment that really tries to change things. Most are ruled by apathy and fear. After this battle, maybe things will change a little." The teams were starting to move up the mountain. Not far up the mountain was a large cave that was supposed to lead to the Temple of Kreaco-Ath. One of the security men had been in it before on a dangerous mission. We climbed a steep trail in single file. We still had packs with food, water, and extra ammunition, and the way was difficult. I could see Jericho's team reaching the cavern, when there was a disturbance. Huge trolls issued out of the cave with clubs. The firing started, and trolls yelled in pain as black blood issued from their wounds. They pressed on with horrible strength, and some of our vanguard was swept from the mountain. However, the firepower of Jericho's team prevailed, and the trolls were destroyed.

"There must be a priest!" yelled Jericho. "Get him quickly before he alerts others to our presence!" He and a few others charged up the mountain and entered the cavern. We all surged forward to help, picking our way through the bodies of the fat trolls. Firing was heard issuing from the confines of the cavern, and flashes of purple light could be seen at other times. When I reached the cavern, I could see Jericho's people firing at a purple globe. There was a priest inside, and he laid about him with a whip from inside the globe, which seemed to be protecting him. None of the rifles could penetrate his shield. The standoff continued for several minutes, when Jericho and some of the others got behind the Borzhat priest. He laid about him furiously with his glowing purple whip, but the small group managed to push the globe out the entrance of the cave. It careened down the side of the mountain, tossing the priest inside all about, until he lost his concentration. Then the globe disappeared, and the priest fell to his death horribly. His crystal was lost down the side of the mountain irretrievably.

"We must press on," said Jericho, "The element of surprise is our best advantage." Jericho and his group led the way into the mountain. There were no other immediate defenses, and the way was clear. The tunnel sloped down further and further, and we turned on the flashlights on the guns. The middle of the way was smooth, as if the feet of a million beings had passed this way before. We traveled long miles spiraling down, until we felt sure that we were below the level of the mountain itself. One time, we ran into a party of trolls and goblins, but we destroyed them quickly, and there was no priest with them. Then the passage opened up into a large cavern. There were many stalactites hanging from the ceiling, multicolored cone shaped objects that had grown over the years. We walked through the cavern gazing around us in wonder, when one of the group stepped on a stone that slid into the ground. A horizontal green light pulsed upward from the floor of the cavern. When it reached the ceiling, the stalactites began to fall with horrible consequences. Many of our group were pierced or crushed by the stone spears. There were cries of pain and dismay echoing through the cavern. Fortunately, the children had not yet entered the cavern with the rearguard, but our section was right in the middle of it. Wolf had avoided the missiles with an animal's sense of danger, but April had had her foot caught under a stone. Other people from Kirsten and Danno's group in Africa had been killed outright. The cavern floor was a mass of rubble, so it was hard to get to the people that were injured. Some couldn't even be moved. Robbins came into the room and took stock of the situation.

"We will leave a rearguard here," he said. "The wounded will stay here with a few able bodied people to protect them. We'll send for help, but we must continue on." Jericho led the way out of the cavern to a new passage that seemed to be the only exit. We all followed him glumly. The passage wound its way down through the mountain. We traveled on slowly, with heavy hearts. Then Jericho and the vanguard stopped in front of us. There was a three-way fork in the passageway. Jericho was determining which way was the best to go. Clearly he did not want to split the teams up in these possibly endless caverns.

"The way stays smooth to the right," he called out. "We will follow the most traveled path." The teams funneled into the right hand passageway, which was quite a bit smaller than the way we had been on. The right hand cavern was rougher and more natural than the previous way. It zigzagged up and down. It seemed to continue father down than up, however, so we went farther into the mountain. Again, we ran into a group of goblins and trolls, and we slaughtered them quickly. They didn't seem to think of running, but rather went into a mindless fury when they saw us. Our superior weaponry brought them down every time. We had some trouble clearing the passageway of bodies. We had to stack them to the side one by one.

Eventually we got through and continued on our way. The passageway opened up into a large cavern with columns. These were fat at the ceiling and floor, and skinny halfway down. They were stalactites that had merged with stalagmites. "Be careful what you step on," called out Jericho, "I doubt there's a trip stone here too, but you never know." There was one obvious entrance out of the cavern, and we started that way, but Jericho called a halt. "The way is rougher here," he called. "This is not the most traveled way." The groups spread out in the cave between the columns, and found the smooth pathway on the ground. It clearly led off to the side, and ended in a wall. Jericho and his vanguard examined the wall, and found a small manufactured crack that outlined a large square. The square was obviously a doorway of some sort, but how could we pass through it? Everyone looked around for a knob of stone that would trip the opening of the door, but there appeared to be nothing.

Finally, Jericho picked the strongest of the security guys, and went up to the door to try to force it open. They pushed and strained to open the door. Their muscles bunched under their shirts, and they grunted with the effort. Then something made a snapping noise, and the

189

stone door slid back and to the side into the wall of the cavern.

Immediately, trolls sprang into the cavern with clubs. The men who had been pushing at the door were all unarmed, and they were taken by surprise. They were strong men, but the trolls were fat giants. The trolls were instantly among the men, and we could not fire into the throng. The men tried to back off, away from the clubs, but the trolls attacked quickly. Wolf sprung to the attack. He pushed the trolls off of our men by leaping at their throats.

Kirsten then yelled out. "Bring the guns in close so we can get a shot! That's the only way." She charged in with her rifle at her shoulder like some kind of professional mercenary. Others followed her. As soon as Wolf caused separation between a troll and a man, the troll was shot at close range. But the security guys were taking losses. Jericho was grappling with a large troll with a helmet. He didn't want to let the troll bring his club into play. But the troll was strong and obtained a bear hug on Jericho. Jericho grimaced as the troll tried to squeeze the life out of him. I stepped in with my rifle and put it right against the trolls shoulder. I pulled the trigger, and the blast tore through the troll. He roared, and loosed Jericho. Jericho pulled out a knife, and buried it to the hilt in the troll's chest. Amazingly, the troll did not die. Black blood spurted from his chest, but he picked up his club and tried to swing. Jericho and I jumped back, and on the follow through, I fired again. The troll fell back to the floor, and I fired several times into his body to make sure he was dead.

While this was going on, two priests had entered

the room. One had a light blue crystal that formed a glowing circle in front of it. The circle was a large shield that warded off bullets from the two priests. The other also had a light blue crystal, and he lobbed small bright globes over the shield with it. The globes exploded when they hit something, like grenades. I instantly went back to get my staff from where I had left it, and took cover behind a column. Pretty much everybody was taking cover behind columns and firing at the duo. Wolf and our group had mostly subdued the trolls, but now the priests were another matter. Several people had been killed by the explosions of the globes, and the shield seemed to adequately protect the two from gunfire. But then, from the side, Robbins and a few of the rearguard fired at the priests. The priests with the light blue crystals were taken unaware, and they were killed in the crossfire. Wolf had torn the throat out of the last troll, and there was quiet in the cavern. Robbins strode to the center of the cavern.

"Jericho," he said, "gather your weapons and men and guard that opening. We'll mop up here." I knew what my job would be. I walked up to the bodies of the priests. Robbins came up with me, and we looked at the dead men. "They're identical twins." Robbins said. "The Borzhat must not have wanted to split them up." I made a noise of assent, and then looked at the crystals. They were a pale light blue, and evil looking. I brought the staff forward, and rested it on one of the crystals. I thought of the wide woods I had been trapped in when I had met Wolf. I also thought of the forest spirit who had released us. I tried to think of the respect and love that I had for those things. The crystal did not break. I thought of the Redwoods of the west and the Baobab trees in Africa. Still the crystal did not break. Usually, the crystal would have broken by this point.

"The crystal is not breaking," I said to Robbins. "There is some resistance."

Robbins replied. "Keep trying. There must be a way." Then I thought of my favorite place, a small wood that had been behind my house as I was growing up. There had been special places in that wood that only I had known about. I had made a map of those places with names for all of the groves and rocks that were distinctive. At this thought the crystal broke. It made small little puddles of light blue liquid, and dissolved into steam. Robbins yelled, "Yes!" and I immediately went to the other crystal. Again, it resisted more than usual, but as I thought of the wood behind my house, it broke. The bodies of the trolls dissolved with the destruction of the final crystal, and a noxious vapor was collecting in the cavern. Robbins took control again. "Alright! Let's line up in our groups and head forward." We organized again and started out of the cavern through the secret door. Jericho and the security guys led the way, and the rest of us followed. The first thing we encountered through the door was another large cavern off to the right that was littered with stools and smelly food. It was obviously a place where the trolls could stay to stand guard, and I guess the Borzhat priests had stayed there too. "This seems to be a good place to spend the night," Robbins said. "We will make mistakes if we go on without sleep. We will set a large watch, because it is likely that more trolls will come through here before the night is over." People were glad as they took off their equipment and supplies. The watch was organized, and I was left out of it entirely. Everyone thought it was fair that I conserve my energy. I bedded down next to Kirsten.

"I think we are making good progress," she said. "No one expected this to be easy."

I was less enthusiastic. "We have fallen for every trap they have set." I said. "If we continue like this there will be no force left to assault the temple itself."

"We have to succeed," she said. "We are the best hope of future generations."

I was tired, and didn't want to argue with the eternal optimist. "Let's just go to sleep and see how tomorrow goes." She agreed, and we got as comfortable as we could. Even on the hard rock, sleep came quickly to me. As I slept, I dreamed.

O Chapter 12

"The offender never pardons."
George Herbert, Jacula Prudentum

My dream began as I fell into a dark bar. It seemed to be one of those places on the edge, where there were people there who were alright, but also some shady people as well. A clear liquid spewed from my mouth, and I felt tired and sick. I felt a presence behind me, and I turned to see what it was. A rough-looking character was coming at me with his arm raised threateningly, but as I turned to see him, he lowered his arm and walked past. Several people were standing at the bar, and others were sitting at tables, so I went up to the bar. That was when I realized that I had bare feet and no wallet. I was convinced that I did not belong in the bar without shoes or money, so I started out the door. However, when I opened the door, I saw that it was very cold outside, and the ground was hard. The rough-looking character was right by my side, and he seemed to welcome me back into the bar. So I closed the door and came back inside.

I went up to the bar again, and asked for a small drink. The bartender filled up a glass halfway and gave it to me kindly. Then, I noticed a rope behind me. It stretched up into a hole in the ceiling. I felt a compulsion to pull on it, and pull I did. A man had been holding onto it, and he fell into the bar with a coil of rope. He collapsed on the floor. People gasped in shock, but I helped him to his feet and patted him on the back. I kind of laughed it off, and some of the other patrons bundled him away. I took my drink and went deeper into the bar. There were a few miniature pool tables lined up against a wall, and I decided to play. I took the tiny colored balls out of the pockets, and started to set them up, when an evil man entered the room. He took one look at me and asked me if I had any ID. My first instinct was to attack him, but a voice in my head told me not to, so I threw some miniature pool balls at him and started to run. I ran out of the bar, but somehow, he was with me. There was a gate ahead that was open, but he was closing it. I tried to force it open, but he was stronger than I. My heart raced, and I felt angry. Then, a calmness overtook me. I concentrated on centering myself, and the gate began to open. At this point, I was shocked into wakefulness.

The lights from the guns were mostly out, and it was dark in the troll's room. I had slept for what seemed a long time, and a muffled scream woke me. I scrambled for my gun, as some others awoke also. I flipped the light on from the gun and swung it around toward the noise. There was nothing there but a footlocker. I looked around, and I noticed that Kirsten was gone. The other people were turning over and going back to sleep, but I called out. "Hey, has anyone seen Kirsten? I think she's gone."

Some people paid attention to me, but others seemed annoyed. "Go to the watch," one said. "Maybe she's just gone off to the bathroom." I had a feeling of trepidation, so I hurried to the watch, which included Wolf. When I asked if they had seen her, they replied in the negative. I went back to the people I was sleeping near. Some of them were shining their lights around the general area in search. I looked at the footlocker that I had focused on earlier. It was not locked, so I opened it. There was absolutely nothing inside. The bottom looked strange, and I knocked on it. It sounded hollow! I clawed at it, searching for purchase, and the bottom pivoted on its hinge and opened. There was a passageway below it, tiny and dark. I called for Robbins and Jericho, and they were found and brought to the passageway. I was looking at it carefully, and I thought that it might be just large enough for Kirsten, but that I would have serious trouble navigating it. There was no way that Jericho or the larger security guys would be able to get down it.

Robbins had been apprised of the situation, and he asked me some questions. "Kirsten is down there? How long has she been gone?"

"I think goblins took her," I said. "She's been gone at least fifteen minutes. Can we go after her?" I already knew the answer to that when I asked it.

"I don't know," Robbins replied. "I think the goblins will have a much easier time traveling down that passageway than any of us would. Even with Kirsten, I imagine they are moving faster than the smallest of us would be able to. Can you get down that passage?"

"I'm not sure," I said. "Kirsten must have been dragged."

"I'd like to go after her, but I don't think it's possible," said Robbins. "Even if someone could get down that tunnel, it would surely be a trap at the end. We just have to accept that they have taken Kirsten. Perhaps they will keep her prisoner."

"We must get to the Temple of Kreaco-Ath as fast as we can," I said. "The less time she spends in their hands, the better chance she will have."

"I agree," said Robbins. Then he yelled out to the rest of the group. "Round 'em up! Get ready to move! We move out in ten minutes." Jericho got his vanguard together, and I found Danno with some of the others of my group. The African children ate something, and a few of them drummed softly, and a thought entered my mind for a moment. The African children could follow after Kirsten in the tunnel. We could give them guns, and they could save her. But I perished the thought. It was stupid and selfish. Sometimes thoughts cross your mind without any way for you to control them. I think that as long as you don't let evil thoughts affect your actions, you're not responsible for them.

Everyone packed up and was ready. We headed down the main passageway that was worn from use. Because of Kirsten's disappearance, we hurried as fast as seemed safe. We traveled through dark passageways. It began to get hotter as we encountered depths we had never reached before. Side passages opened occasionally, but we followed the most traveled way. Then Jericho called a halt. There were two passages that were well traveled. A security man reported that one of the passages entered a large cavern. Jericho decided to enter this one.

I can barely describe my reaction to the amazing sight we beheld. As we entered, the lights from the guns were reflected back on us a thousand fold. There were veins of clear crystal running all through the walls of the huge space. They continued into the ceiling and floor. In addition, runes of reddish black were painted all over any space that was not shot through with crystal. The crystal veins seemed to lead to a pedestal that was in the center of the cavern. They spiraled up the rock of the pedestal and led to a bowl in the top of it. There didn't seem to be any exits, but we had been fooled before, so we searched diligently. Everyone entered the cavern.

Then, there was a flickering light in the bowl in the top of the pedestal. Grey smoke poured out and spilled over the sides. It collected at the bottom of the pedestal, and then seemed to achieve a life of its own. A mass of smoke flew around the room, looking like a dark comet. It fetched up in a corner of the room, and everyone backed away from it, guns at the ready. The grey smoke coalesced into the form of a grey robed man, with a grey crystal in his hand. Instantly, several people fired, but a globe of grey light appeared around him. Bullets were heard hitting rock, and several people cried out in pain. The priest stretched out his hand, and smoke poured forth. It split into five segments and came into our group of people. The smoke bunched up in five separate places and pupated into horrible creatures. They had round heads with jaws filled with horrible teeth. These heads bobbed and hung from snake-like necks that were attached to spiny bodies. The bodies were fat and slow, but quickly the heads stretched out and started biting at people. The first monster had already struck and bitten into the entire head of one of our security men. The firing began, and screams of pain and panic were heard. Both Jericho and Robbins were desperately trying to coordinate a defense to these monsters. The priest just stood in the corner and waved his glowing crystal in a circle. Bullets seemed to have no effect on the monsters, and they kept striking at our party. Everyone was trying to stay well back of them, but they each had a sphere of influence in the room. Then Jericho unsheathed his knife and leaped at one of the monsters. He plunged his knife into the chest of the creature, and seemed to be swallowed up into its body. Just then, I felt a tug at my shirt.

A small African child was behind me, and he pointed to a corner of the room where there was no action going on. A grey robed priest was standing there with a grey crystal in his hand. He looked to be a twin of the priest that had come out of the smoke, but this one had no shield around him. There were a few people between me and the priest, and I didn't have a clear shot, so I started running in his direction. He seemed to be concentrating on the action until I came near to him and raised my gun. He lifted his crystal and seemed to displace five paces to the right. I heard Jericho yelling for everyone to stop firing, but I raised my gun and fired at the grey robed priest. He seemed to be immune to my bullets, and a suspicion took hold of my mind. I fired again, this time at the spot where he had been before, and he yelled. His image appeared in front of me where it had been, and the other image disappeared. Cries of amazement were heard around the room, but I was concentrating on the priest. I fired again, and he dropped his crystal on the ground. Several people were now looking in our direction, and I kicked the crystal away from him.

Then, Robbins was at the scene. "Grey robes?" He asked of the priest. "This is new. Who are you?"

The priest snarled in reply. "Yes, I am Mezra Donell, one of the high priests, and master of illusion. You have discovered my secret, but the other two high priests of

Kreaco-Ath will slay you all." I looked around the room, and there were no monsters, no other Borzhat priests, only men and women from our own group hurt and dying from stray bullets.

Robbins spoke again. "What are the powers of the other high priests? Tell us." The master of illusion just scrambled for his crystal, but we easily pushed him back. Robbins looked at me. "Get ready to destroy the crystal if he doesn't talk," he said. I put the tip of my staff on the crystal and thought of the forest lightly. The priest grimaced, but said nothing. "Destroy it," said Robbins. "We don't have time for this." I again thought of beautiful trees and places I had known, and soon the crystal was destroyed. The priest turned a chalky grey color, and melted into a pool of slime that evaporated quickly.

Then we looked around the room. There were a few people that were dead, and a dozen at least were wounded. Some clearly couldn't continue. Robbins looked heavenward and asked, "Why didn't we bring a doctor?" Then he organized the people that were hurt. "Most of you must go back to the cavern where the other wounded are. If you can't make it, I guess you'll just have to stay here, but we are close now. You'll be in a lot of danger here. The rest of us most press on. No more mistakes!" The wounded bound up their wounds and tried to help each other get ready to go back. The rest of us, about twenty-five besides the children, got ready to move on. Each group went their separate ways.

Jericho led the way down the other fork in the caverns, and we trailed out behind him. The path flattened out a little, and the rock became black. We went on for quite a way when we saw a red glow in front of us. The heat became oppressive, and we entered a cavern larger than any other. It seemed almost as if we had come out into the open sky, so large was this cavern. All around us was a lake of fire, magma flowing and churning. A long arching bridge led from our landing to an island in the middle of lake. On the island was a series of manufactured and natural towers. It looked something like a gigantic sand drip castle. The towers looked like minarets, and were connected with soaring walkways with crenellations. Embrasures spotted the lower walls. A cavernous entrance to this structure opened opposite the bridge across the lake. There appeared to be no portcullis or other impediment to the entrance. We gathered at the beginning of the slender bridge across the lake of lava.

"We must cross quickly and enter the castle," Robbins said. "Surely this is our final destination." Jericho and the other leaders agreed, so we began to cross the bridge. Soon we were traveling two by two, as the bridge narrowed dangerously. The heat from the lava was making us all extremely uncomfortable. The bridge had no hand rails or walls, so we could look over the side right into the lava. The glow from the lava gave plenty of red light for us to see by. We made it to the highest point of the bridge. As yet, there was no outcry from the castle. It was sure that they knew we were coming by this time, but no one appeared on the battlements. Jericho and the vanguard made it to the island, and the rest of us followed. They flattened themselves against the walls of the monstrous castle and headed toward the entrance. Jericho entered the huge opening, and waved us on. We all ran inside, and took stock of the situation. There was a large courtyard inside, with multiple levels of balconies stretching high toward the ceiling. As we were looking around at this, a creaking and rattling of chains sounded from behind us. There was a portcullis! It fell with a booming crash to the ground, sealing us in the castle. We looked around for an enemy, as the echoes from the sound rebounded throughout the space. No one appeared at this moment. Jericho looked around and shrugged. Apparently, one way seemed as good as another to him, and he started off to the left.

We went through corridors lit with strange clear crystals. They were mounted on brackets in the walls, and they gave off a cool clear light. There were mosaics depicting horrible human sacrifices, and battles where crystals figured prominently. There were huge rugs hanging from the ceiling, intricately woven. Suits of armor and statues stood in alcoves. A massive mirror hung from a wall, with beautiful gold trim. Everywhere, there was evidence of wealth and power, but no one appeared to be in the castle. We entered rooms that led to other corridors. These rooms had ornate couches and tables, paintings of demons and devils. One painting in particular struck me. It seemed to be a very old oil painting. There were tiny cracks in the surface of the paint on the canvas. It was a portrait of a dull eyed albino man with a glowing crystal in his forehead. It seemed to be an exact duplicate of the golem! We continued on through the rooms and corridors.

At the end of one large corridor was a set of double doors. Jericho took the vanguard through the doors, and the rest of us followed. The room was a large amphitheatre. There were large crystal chandeliers that gave light from the ceiling. It had large rock steps for sitting on, and smaller ones for getting closer to the stage at the front. We had filed into the room and were walking down the small steps, when a man with yellow robes walked on to the stage from the side.

"Welcome to Kreaco-Ath," he said in a loud voice, projecting it for his audience. "It is true you have us at a disadvantage. Had we known you were coming, we would have filled the castle with men to greet you." Wolf looked at me and growled, and I said, "I'll bet." The yellow robed man continued. "I extend our felicitations to your group, and I offer a deal. We will let our pretty guest with the red hair return with you to the surface. We will help all your wounded as much as we are able. All you have to do is hand over the staff that the young man holds there."

Robbins replied. "Where are you holding Kirsten? We want to see her."

The man in yellow robes smiled. "All in good time. She is safe where she is. Why don't you just decide whether you agree to our terms?"

Robbins looked around at our group, and then he looked back at the man in yellow robes. "We do not agree!" He shouted. As one, the guns were raised, but the man in yellow robes pulled a yellow crystal from his sleeve at the same time.

"I am the Lord of Chaos!" He shouted. "Feel my wrath!" Small wiry goblins burst into the room from doors at the sides, and the yellow crystal was raised. A few people fired, but the stage was not close enough, and it seemed that everyone missed. The crystal pulsed with a yellow light, and the world changed.

*　*　*　*　*

A burst of bright yellow light blinded me, but then, I saw colors of every kind. It was as if I had been rubbing my eyes for a long time, and swirls of different color encircled me. The amphitheatre was gone, only the colors remained. There were red lightening bolts with rainbow afterimages. These were followed by bouncing blue circles. The sounds had gone crazy as well. Mostly there was static, but whistles and explosions came at me from every direction. If you've ever heard the song Revolution #9 off of the Beatles White Album, you'll have some idea of what I was hearing, but this was a thousand times worse. And the colors continued. Hula hoops spun and broke apart in green and black and cyan. Spinning lines of dark blue and purple skittered beneath my feet, but I felt that I was weightless. The floor and seats were gone. I was all alone.

Straight neon green lines flashed and spun. Yellow sparklers appeared and disappeared. I was starting to feel sick, and I couldn't see anyone. Red columns came in from the sides and crowded me. All of this disappeared and reappeared as fast as I could focus on it. The sounds continued. A door's creaking was predominant, but a hundred times louder. Then the static overwhelmed again, as it gained and reduced in volume. It sounded like a radio that was almost finding a station, but it never quite did. It seemed to go on for hours, as my sense of time was lost. Then I heard a faint drumming. It was somehow familiar and different from the rest of the chaos. The drumming became more regular, and grew in volume. The chaos around me weakened for a moment, and then desperately became even wilder. But the drumming continued, and it was something to hold on to. Like a rope that is being dragged behind a ship, I held on, buffeted by the chaos. Then, shreds of reality peeked through the madness. I could see the amphitheatre! The drumming was coming from the African children. And the goblins were advancing, even reaching the front of our group.

We retaliated in a hail of gunfire. The goblins were thrown back. Someone had taken a shot at the priest in yellow robes, and he was distracted. The chaos ended. We surged down the steps, mowing through the goblins. The yellow priest turned to leave, but Wolf had run ahead of the vanguard. With one leap, Wolf gained the stage. He tackled the priest with his full weight and bore him to the ground. Wolf's jaws closed on the hand that held the crystal, and the priest cried out in pain. The rest of us fought off the goblins until they fled, and we mounted the stage.

The priest was struggling, but Wolf had him pinned. Jericho put a gun to his head and barked some questions. "Where is Kirsten? Where is your hostage?" The priest shook his head and tried to activate his crystal. I knocked it away with the staff as Wolf clamped down on the hand. Jericho tried a different tack. "Where is the last high priest? What are his powers?"

The yellow priest smiled. "The highest priest will give your blood to the primus crystal, and you will all become part of our power."

Robbins shouted in anger. "Destroy the crystal! We will find her ourselves." Wolf released the man's hand and wrapped his huge jaws around his throat and growled menacingly. I touched the staff to the yellow crystal and thought of my favorite forested places. Again, the crystal resisted destruction immediately. It was as if the closer we got to the primus crystal, the more strength the crystals had. Eventually the crystal succumbed to my thoughts of greener places, and it was split into shards. The high priest in yellow robes yelled for a final time and expired. He dissolved into a yellow steam slowly.

Wolf stepped away from the body and looked up at me with a strange look in his eyes. "To have one's senses taken away," he said. "That is the most horrible nightmare one could endure. Smell, Hearing, Sight… all gone. How could one man have such power?" He seemed profoundly changed by the experience, almost as if he had known fear for the first time in his life.

I scratched him behind his ears and tried to comfort him. "You brought him down, Wolf. You and the African children." I glanced over at the leadership of the group. Robbins was talking heatedly with Jericho and others. He noticed my glance and waved me over.

"I don't think we're going to be able to save Kirsten," he said. "We just don't know where she is being held. We have to try to make it straight to the primus crystal. If we can destroy that before Kirsten is killed…" He trailed off.

Jericho took charge. "It's time to move. Conversation doesn't get us anywhere." He rounded up the vanguard and scouted stage left. Everyone regrouped and followed him. Wolf stayed close to me. We went past some curtains, and then through an open entrance that brought us to a long hallway. After some twists and turns, we found some flights of stairs going up. We were forced to stretch our column thin to get through this series of passages, and we were constantly aware of our vulnerability to attack. After the stairs, we passed along an open balcony high above a courtyard. A giant tower loomed over the courtyard, and in a window in the highest part of the tower, we could see gleams of multicolored light. A general halt was called, and everyone became aware of the light show going on in the tower. Jericho glanced around the courtyard and saw where our passage seemed to connect with the tower. He moved back up to the front and waved us ahead. We continued around the balcony until we came to the stairs to the tower. In order to climb the stairs, we had to pass beneath two large statues. They were statues of men, reaching high in the air to hold hands, forming an arch.

Robbins came up from the rearguard and pulled me to the front. "This will be the final confrontation," he said. "I need you and Wolf to be here with me in the vanguard." We looked warily at the statues, but entered the tower. The spiral stone staircase hugged the outside wall of the tower. The way was lit by red crystal sconces every so often, leaving us in a sickly semi-light. We walked two by two up the stairs.

The climb seemed endless. The stairs went on and on, but did not narrow appreciably. The tower was hollow, and the empty space to our left yawned open. It was a vertiginous climb, because the red light showed the fall all the way to the bottom. We continued our way up the tower. Eventually, the stairs reached a trap door in the ceiling.

Jericho whispered quietly to us. "The vanguard goes through, no one else. We don't want to get too crowded."

The vanguard consisted of eight people including Wolf and me. Jericho continued. "On the count of three now; one… two… THREE!" He burst through the door, and the others followed him, climbing up as best they could.

When I entered the room, I saw several things over the backs of my comrades. The first thing that dominated the room was the great multicolored crystal on a dais near the far end of the room. The crystal was super-faceted, and every facet was a different color. It glowed with evil, and the glow seemed to pulse in time with a heart beat. A priest wearing an ornate crown stood above the crystal, the life pouring out of his veins. Blood from his wrists poured down on to the crystal, where it was absorbed. It seemed the flow of his blood was slowing to a stop, although the huge gashes in his wrists and forearms looked as if they would bleed more. The priest held a curved knife in one hand, and a black crystal in the other. Then, near him, I saw,

"Kirsten!" I yelled. She was held around the neck by a huge troll. The troll would easily snuff her life before we could make any move on the priest or the troll himself. The vanguard stood at the ready, with weapons raised as the priests blood slowed to a trickle. The last of his blood poured out on to the crystal, and he put his wrists down slowly. He let out a soft sigh, and a strange black glow surrounded him. The primus crystal pulsed more slowly, and then faded to a soft glow as well.

"I am old and bored," The priest said quietly. "The great tedium that is life, or death, no longer excites me in any way. You think I am evil? No, it is the boredom that permeates my very being that causes you to think this about me. Control is the only thing I can cling to. If others are as miserable as I am, I no longer feel so alone. I must own everything, even though the most special of possessions does not matter to me. There is one thing that might lift my spirits, however." He paused and looked straight at me. "That staff. For so long it has eluded me. Do you want your friend here to live? I will give her to you if you hand the staff over to me."

"Never!" I said. "You destroyed my home. I will never give in to your desires." But Robbins nudged me to silence. He spoke to the high priest.

"Well then, what if we make the exchange simultaneously? We will put the staff down between us, and you release Kirsten to us." The high priest nodded solemnly.

"You are wise, leader of men. That is the only way your friend will stay alive." Robbins nodded to me, and the high priest gestured at the troll. Very carefully we approached the center of the room. I put the staff on the floor but stayed close. The priest advanced, and the troll held Kirsten at arms length. The priest motioned for me to back away, and I did slowly. As the priest got closer to the staff, the troll released Kirsten's neck.

"No!" She cried, as she ran to us. The priest swooped down on the staff and grabbed it with the hand that held the knife.

"Fire!" Robbins cried, and the tower room resounded with the sound of gunfire. All of the rounds were concentrated on the priest, and he was flung back against the primus crystal. The troll roared and charged, and the guns swung to cover him. Bullets slammed into him and he fell to the ground with his arms outstretched toward us. Then a cackling laugh was heard. The high priest lurched to his feet and held the intricately carved staff in the air. He pointed his black crystal at the staff, and the staff erupted into flame. It quickly disintegrated into ash, and the grey powder floated to the floor. The priest laughed again and pointed the crystal at us. The vanguard fired again, and he was thrown back against a wall. He slumped to the floor, but then put his hand on the wall and crawled to his feet again.

"Don't you see?" He said. "I have given my life to the crystal. I cannot die so long as it lives. And now that the staff is destroyed, I have achieved immortality!" Wolf growled and leaped at the high priest, but the priest swung the black crystal in his hand to bear. A black lance of light stabbed at Wolf and threw him back. Wolf's coat burst into flame, and he howled in pain. I threw myself on him trying to smother the flames. At that moment, Jericho fired a shot at the priest. Not at the man himself, but at the black crystal he held. It was the perfect shot. The crystal went spinning out of his hands, and one of the other men in the vanguard stood over it with his gun at the ready. The priest stood behind the primus crystal and put his hand on it. He passed his hand over several different facets and then seemed to decide on one, a deep red crystal. He raised his knife and plunged it into the primus crystal. The deep red crystal pulled free, and the priest raised it high.

Our small vanguard reloaded and fired again. The high priest pointed the crystal at us, and a translucent red globe appeared from the crystal. It swelled quickly to fill the room. The priest was knocked back by the bullets, but this time, he stayed on his feet. I started toward him, but noticed that my movements were restricted, as if I moved through syrup. Time had slowed for us. The priest turned to look at the man standing over his black crystal. The man showed his fear of the priest, albeit slowly. He fired several times, but now the priest was out of the line of fire and advancing. But Wolf was on his feet! He leaped straight toward the crystal, but it was obvious that his time had been slowed as well. The high priest's circuitous route, and Wolf's slower straight one brought them to the crystal at the same time. Wolf locked his jaws on the black crystal, and the priest stabbed at him with his knife. The knife left a deep gash on his flank, along with all the horrible burns that already scored his back.

Others in the vanguard were still firing, and their aim was able to catch up finally. The priest was flung back against a wall. The syrupy feel was starting to dissipate, and I headed toward the primus crystal. The firing pinned the priest against the back wall, and the vanguard advanced. The priest raised his deep red crystal again, and a red sphere again filled the room. We were caught up in the slowed time effects the priest had enacted. Wolf was the quickest of us, and he tossed the black crystal in Jericho's direction and leapt to the attack. He bounded slowly across the room as people fired into the priest keeping him off balance. I reached the primus crystal at the same time that Wolf reached the priest. The firing tapered off as Wolf's body blocked clear shots at the priest. The high priest stabbed at Wolf with the knife, and his jeweled crown slipped over one eye. However, Wolf was inside the priest's reach, and his jaws clamped down on the knife arm. My arms encircled

211

the primus crystal as the priest raised his red crystal. Spheres of deep red bathed the room, and time slowed quickly. At first, movement was possible, but as more spheres pulsed out of the crystal, time stopped. The priest tugged at his arm with the knife, but Wolf's jaws remained locked. It was a deadlock. The priest was helpless in Wolf's grasp, but none of us could move a muscle.

The high priest yelled in anger and straightened his crown. He beat at Wolf with the hand that held the crystal, and he kept the translucent globes of slow time coming. My palms were on the primus crystal, and I did the only thing I could do. I thought of private glens in the woods I had been to after hiking for hours. I thought of the woods behind my house that I had played in as a child. I thought of the elusive forest spirit that had visited us in the endless forest. This thought lingered in my mind and appeared to achieve a life of its own.

"The primus crystal is not evil." The forest spirit said. "It is simply a power as there are other powers in the universe. It has been perverted with blood and knife to serve the uses of evil masters." Bark closed up over the spirit's face. I tried to think of all different kinds of forests and trees that I had seen, but still the crystal stayed indifferent to my thoughts. I heard the priest snarling and swearing in Wolf's grasp, and I thought of Wolf. I could see he was hurting, perhaps worse even than the time he was in the forest when I found him. I thought of the time that he had saved Kirsten in the jail, and the many times he had saved us all. For one time in my life I knew I had a true friend in Wolf, and I wanted to tell him now. At this, the crystal began to shake in my hands. At first it was just a small vibration, but it grew stronger and stronger. The facets and pieces began to fall apart and fall to the ground. There they hissed and steamed like water on a frying pan. Hundreds of different colored crystals were falling and jumping and turning into steam. Even the black crystal and the deep red crystal in the priest's hand were melting. Time speeded back up to its normal velocity, and Jericho and the vanguard advanced on the priest. But there was no need. The priest began to dissolve and mutate. Instead of turning into steam, his body became thousands and thousands of little red ants. Wolf sprang back, and the ants crawled for the cracks in the flagstones of the room. There was a whole mound of them, so it took some time, but slowly, they all disappeared into the edges and corners of the room. Jericho had stepped on a few, but there were so many that it didn't seem to matter much. Robbins clapped me on the back and congratulated me heartily. I stepped over to Wolf first, and looked at his wounds. Wolf looked up at me tiredly, and I looked straight into his eyes.

"You've been a good friend to me Wolf," I said. "I hope we will always be together." He didn't answer directly, but he put his nose under my hand and pushed it up so I could scratch behind his ears. Then Kirsten came running over and gave me a big hug.

"I'm so glad that you came to save me," she said. "They said they were going to do horrible things to all of us." I was conscious of how much she had helped us along this journey, and I hugged her back.

"Things will be better now, you'll see," I said to her. She smiled back in return. Everyone else was cheering and yelling. The news was passed down through the trap door to the others, and the African children began drumming wildly. Robbins took it upon himself to make a speech.

"A great evil has been stopped here today. Not all of you will have a home to go to after this fight. But all of us will find a new start somewhere. Let us not be complacent and believe that because of this victory we can rest on our laurels forever. But it is true that you only have to save the world once!" Everyone cheered at that, and Robbins continued. "Let us bring the news to our wounded, and help them back to the surface." We all gathered together and made our way back down the tower. Soon we were helping our wounded travel back to the outside world and our initial location where the Dugouts had left their instruments. We all gathered there in front of the stage, and although the band seemed tired, they got on stage to take us away from this godforsaken place. They played a few songs, and the mountains faded. We appeared in a city on the same world, the same location as the festival that we had been at so long before. Kirsten danced happily because she was home, and most of the group mingled in with a new crowd that had formed all around us. The wounded were taken to a nearby hospital, and it seemed that this place was now inviting and friendly to us all.

❖ Epilogue

"There is something in October sets the gypsy blood astir."
Bliss Carman, A Vagabond Song

Kirsten and I had adopted two of the African children. Kirsten had sort of adopted me, as I didn't have a home to go to. We figured it was better if the children had a home with us rather than going to an orphanage. Wolf was staying with us too. For two months, it had been going fairly well, but now Wolf seemed restless. He wasn't getting enough time outside, so we decided to talk about it after dinner. Kirsten started the conversation.

"Wolf, we've seen that you're not happy here," she said. Wolf lowered his head and said nothing. "We don't want to force you to stay with us. Just decide what you want to do, and we'll do anything we can to make you happy." Wolf still said nothing. I crouched next to him and put my head close to his ear.

"We'll always be friends, Wolf. You don't have to stay to prove that. Just tell us what you want." Wolf lowered his head even more and spoke for the first time.

"It is time for me to move on. I have discharged my obligations to you for saving me. You know it is more than that, though. I cannot be contained in this small space forever. I wish you were all wolves so I could take you with me, but now, I must go to the forest." Our two adopted children came around and hugged him, for he had been their constant companion and guardian for the two months that he had stayed with us. I stood and turned away for a moment. I had known it was coming, but it was hard to take all the same. Kirsten also came and gave him a hug, and Wolf licked her face.

"I'll take him," I said. "Tomorrow, in the morning, we'll go to the national forest." We took our after-dinner walk around the neighborhood. Neighbors went inside when we went around, and they peeked through windows around drawn curtains. It was a somber walk, silent but for the evening birds. There was a beautiful sunset, made even nicer with clouds above it. We watched the sun as it seemed to disappear so quickly, as things coming to an end often do. Then we went back inside Kirsten's house. The silence continued there, until it was time for bed. We all said goodnight to each other, and tried to go to sleep.

Early in the morning, I awoke before the others. I went into the living room where Wolf slept. He was already awake and pacing the room. We went out quietly to the van, and started the drive to the national forest. It was a three hour drive to a trail we had gone to several times, and the time was spent in silence again. When we reached the trailhead, we parked and got out. Wolf sat down and looked up at me and I looked at him.

"I never thought I'd lose you," I said. "Not once the danger was over." Wolf replied.

"You have Kirsten and the children now. You don't need me any more."

"I do need you!" I yelled, and I grabbed him around the neck in a terrific hug.

"Perhaps that is so," he said emotionally. After awhile, I let go, and he turned and headed up the trail. When he came to the top of a rise, he stopped, and turned and looked back. Then he gave a terrific howl, and headed

217

deeper into the forest, lost to my sight. I waited for awhile, but the forest was quiet. I got back in the van and began the long drive home.